# The High School Boys' Fishing Trip

## H. Irving Hancock

# Contents

# THE HIGH SCHOOL BOYS' FISHING TRIP

BY

H. Irving Hancock

# CHAPTER I
# TOM READE HAS A "BRAND-NEW ONE"

Hello, Timmy!"

"'Lo, Reade."

"Warm night," observed Tom Reade, as he paused not far from the street corner to wipe his perspiring face and neck with his handkerchief.

"Middling warm," admitted Timmy Finbrink.

Yet the heat couldn't have made him extremely uncomfortable, for Tom Reade, amiable and budding senior in the Gridley High School, smiled good naturedly as he stood surveying as much as he could make out of the face of Timmy Finbrink in that dark stretch of the street.

Timmy was merely a prospective freshman, having been graduated a few days before from the North Grammar School in Gridley.

Tom, himself, had been graduated, three years before, from the fine old Central Grammar, whence, in his estimation, all the "regular" boys came. As a North Grammar boy, Timmy was to be regarded only with easygoing indifference. Yet a tale of woe quickly made Tom Reade his young fellow citizen's instant ally.

"Aren't you out pretty late, Timmy, for a boy who isn't even a regular high school freshman as yet?" inquired Reade, with another smile. "It's almost nine-thirty, you know."

"Don't I know?" wailed Timmy Finbrink, with something of a shiver. "It's getting later every minute, too, and I'm due for a trouncing when I do go in, so what's the odds?"

"Who's going to give you that trouncing?" Tom demanded.

"My father," replied Timmy Finbrink.

"What have you been doing?"

"Pop told me to be upstairs and in bed by nine o'clock, without fail," Timmy explained. "I came along just five minutes ago, and found that pop has the house planted for me. I can't slip in without his knowing it."

"Oho! So your father has the other members of the family stationed where they can see you, whichever way you go into the house?" asked Reade, with genuine interest in the unfortunate Timmy.

"Nope," explained Timmy, with another shiver. "Mother and sister are away visiting, and pop is all alone in the house."

"But he can't watch both the front and back doors at the same time," Reade suggested hopefully.

"Can't he do just that, though?" sputtered Timmy. "I've been scouting on tiptoe around the house to get the lay of the land. Pop is smoking his pipe, and has placed his chair so that he can see both the back and the front doors, for he has the room doors open right through. There isn't a ghost of a show to get in without being seen---and pop has the strap on a chair beside him!" finished Timmy, with an anticipatory shiver.

"Timmy, you're a fearfully slow boy," Tom drawled.

"What do you mean?"

"I can fix it so you can get into the house while your father is doing something else," Tom declared.

"Can you? How? Ring the front door bell, while I slip in at the back door?"

"Nothing as stale as that," scoffed Tom Reade. "That wouldn't call for any brains, you see. Come along and we'll look over the lay of the land. Cheer up, Timmy! You'll have plenty of chance to slip into the house, get upstairs, undressed and be in bed before your father has time to get over the surprise that's coming to him."

"What are you going to-----" Timmy began breathlessly, but Tom interrupted him with:

"Keep quiet, and be ready to follow orders fast."

As they gained the front gate of the Finbrink yard Tom's keen eyes noted a brick lying on the grass. As that was just what he wanted, he pounced upon it.

"Now, Timmy, do you know where you can find a fairly good-sized bottle---without going into the house or taking the risk of being seen by your father?"

"Yes; there's one back of the house, with the ashes," Timmy answered eagerly.

"Go and get it, and don't make any noise."

Timmy disappeared in the darkness beyond, but soon returned carrying an empty quart bottle.

"Good enough!" whispered Reade, eyeing the bottle with cordial interest. Then he noiselessly approached the house, laying the brick on the grass under one of the front windows.

"Now, Timmy, you slip around to the back of the house," whispered the young schemer. "Just as soon as you hear a crash you watch your swiftest chance to slip into the house and upstairs to bed. Understand?"

"Sure! What you-----"

"Don't stop to ask questions. Get on your mark and look out for your own best interests!"

Rejoicing in the possession of such a valuable ally as Tom Reade, Timmy vanished in the darkness. Tom Reade waited until he judged that the youngster must be in position near the back door. Now Tom gripped the bottle in his left hand, crouching over the brick.

With his felt hat in his right hand, Tom reached up, hitting a window pane smartly with the hat. At the same instant he brought the bottle crashing down over the brick.

As the bottle smashed against the brick Mr. Finbrink, in the dining room of the house, jumped up so quickly that he dropped his pipe.

"Some young rascal has smashed a front window!" he gasped, as he bolted into the parlor.

That was just what the noise had sounded like, and Tom Reade had intended that it should do so.

"I'll catch the young scamp!" gasped Mr. Finbrink, making a rush for the front door, which he pulled open.

Pausing an instant, he heard the sound of running feet in the distance.

"The young scoundrel went west, and he has a good start," grunted Mr. Finbrink, as he gave chase in that direction. "Hang it, I don't believe I can catch him!"

That guess proved well founded. After running a short distance Mr. Finbrink halted. He had not caught sight of the fugitive, nor could he now hear the running steps.

"I wonder how many panes of glass the young scamp broke?" muttered the irate Mr. Finbrink.

Retracing his steps quickly, Mr. Finbrink halted in front of his house, scanning the windows. Not a crack in a window pane could he discern, which was not remarkable, in view of the fact that no panes of glass had been broken.

"I need a lantern," Mr. Finbrink said to himself, and went inside the house. Soon afterwards he came out with a lighted lantern, and began his inspection. Three windows showed no sign of damage. Nor did the fourth. Then  Mr.  Finbrink chanced to glance down at the ground. There rested the brick, the fragments of the broken bottle lying around it.

"Say, what's that? What's that?" ejaculated Mr. Finbrink, much puzzled. Soon, however, he began to see light on the riddle. His lips parted in a grin; the grin became a chuckle.

"Humph! That goes ahead of anything I ever had the brains to think up when I was a boy," laughed the man. "That's a good one! It sounded for all the world as though someone had smashed one of my windows with a brick-bat. Ha, ha, ha! That's an all right one! I'd be willing to shake hands with the boy who put up that joke on me. How about my own Timmy, I wonder? No; Timmy wouldn't be smart enough for this one---but he may have smart friends. I'll look up that young hopeful of mine!"

With that purpose in view, the lantern still in his hand, Mr. Finbrink passed into the house and then up the back stairs. On the next floor he pushed open the door of a room, holding the lantern high as he scanned the bed.

There lay Master Timmy, covered only with a sheet, his head sunk in the depths of a pillow, eyes tightly closed, and breathing with almost mechanical rhythm.

"Oh, you're asleep, aren't you?" demanded his father, in a low, ironical voice. "How long have you been asleep, Tim?"

But Timmy's only answer was the beginning of a snore.

"Are you very tired, Timmy?" continued his father craftily.

Still no answer.

Mr. Finbrink held the lantern so that the rays shone fully against the boy's closed eyelids. Any youngster genuinely asleep would have opened his eyes instantly, and Mr. Finbrink knew it. But Timmy began to snore in earnest.

"I'm glad you sleep so soundly," went on Mr. Finbrink. "It shows, boy, what a clear conscience you have! No guile in your heart! But I wish you'd wake up and tell me who broke the bottle against the brick and made me sprint down the street."

Still young Master Timmy snored.

"In your sleeve you're laughing, to think how you fooled your father, aren't you?" murmured Mr. Finbrink. "Well, it was a good joke, and I admit it, young man, so I'm not going to trounce you this time. But I'd be glad if you'd wake up and tell me who put you up to that game."

Master Timmy, however, was disobliging enough to slumber on.

"All right, then," nodded the father. "I say again, it was a good joke. Good night!"

Only a little louder snore served as the son's answer. Mr. Finbrink went out, closed the door and his footsteps sounded down the hallway.

"Whew!" gasped Master Timmy, opening his eyes presently. "That was a mighty narrow squeak! But I got out of it this time. That Tom Reade is a sure enough wonder!"

Mr. Finbrink, however, had slipped back, catfooted, and was now outside the door, where he could hear the barely audible mutterings of his son and heir.

"So it was Tom Reade, eh?" murmured Mr. Finbrink, as he started for the stairs in earnest this time. "I might have guessed it was Tom Reade. He has genius enough for even greater things than that. But Timmy has certainly helped, at least, to earn a right not to be strapped this time." Then the father returned to his chair downstairs, to resume his interrupted smoke. Within the next half hour Mr. Finbrink chuckled many a time over the remembrance of the pranks of his boyhood days.

"But we had no Tom Reade in *our* crowd in those good old days," he repeated to himself several times. "If we had had a Tom Reade among us, I think we would have beaten any crowd of boys of to-day!"

Meanwhile Tom's love of mischief was speeding him into other experiences ere he reached his bed that night. Some of the consequences of his mischievous prank were to be immediate, others more remote.

"Humph! But that did sound just like a window breaking," Tom chuckled as he slowed down to a walk. "Whee! I'd like to show that one to Dick Prescott. I wonder if he is up yet?"

Whereupon Tom walked briskly over to the side street, just off Main Street, whereon stood the book store of Prescott, Senior, with the Prescotts' living rooms overhead.

"Good evening, Mr. Prescott. Good evening, Mrs. Prescott," was Tom's greeting as he walked into the store. "Is Dick up yet?"

"He went upstairs not more than two minutes ago," Mrs. Prescott replied. "He can't be asleep yet. Shall I call upstairs to see?"

"On second thought, perhaps not," Tom replied. "Thank you, just as much. But I've something new that I'd like to show Dick. Do you mind if I slip out around the back of the store and try a new trick on him? It won't hurt anyone; there'll be a crash of glass, but it won't break any good glass---merely a bottle."

"I think that perhaps our son needs a little enlivening," smiled Mr. Prescott.

"Thank you," answered Tom. "You won't be startled, will you, Mrs. Prescott?"

"I don't see how I can possibly be startled, when I've been so kindly warned," laughed Mrs. Prescott.

Then, as Reade darted from the store, Mrs. Prescott added, to her husband:

"I think the back of Tom Reade's head contains more pranks than that of any other boy I ever knew."

"I don't imagine our own son is any too far behind him," replied Mr. Prescott dryly.

A minute or two passed. Then there sounded under one of the store's rear windows a most realistic crash of glass. With it mingled another sound, not so easy to determine, followed by a loud yell and the noise of running feet. Now, out in the street the cry sounded:

"There he goes! Get him!"

"Throw him down and hold him!" yelled another voice.

"Mercy!" gasped Mrs. Prescott.

"Don't be alarmed, my dear," smiled Mr. Prescott. "It's only the natural aftermath of Tom Reade's newest startler."

Was it?

Dick Prescott, after yawning twice, and before starting to disrobe, had decided that his adjustable screen was not fixed in the window of his bedroom as securely as it should be. In endeavoring to fix it he found it necessary to remove the screen from the window. Hardly had he done so when, gazing down into the darkness, he saw a dimly visible figure flitting over the ground below.

"Who's that?" murmured Dick to himself. "What's up?"

Whoever the prowler was, he was flitting over to the ash cans set out by a neighbor. One can contained ashes only, the other contained various kinds of rubbish. It took the prowler but a moment to find an empty bottle in the second can. Then he came straight over toward the rear window of the store, which was situated directly under Dick's own window.

"There's some mischief afloat," murmured Dick, unable to recognize his chum in the darkness. "I can't get down in time to catch him, but I'll mark him so that I'll know him when I overtake him."

Tip-toeing over to his washstand, Dick quickly picked up the water pitcher. He returned to his window just as Tom crouched under the store window with a bottle in his left hand and his felt hat in his right.

Then Tom struck the harmless blow against the window, at the same time breaking the bottle.

Smash!

Splash!

"Gracious!" gasped Dick, believing that the store window had been broken.

A yell from Tom arose as the contents of the pitcher deluged him.

Reade was up and away like a shot, reaching the street only to cause a hue and cry to be started after him as he ran.

So swiftly had Tom moved, that by the time Dick Prescott reached the street both pursuers and pursued were a block away and going fast. Dick was about to join the chase when his father called after him:

"Dick! Dick! Come back here!"

"Yes, sir," replied young Prescott, halting, wheeling, then springing back. "But that scoundrel smashed the rear store window!"

"No, he didn't," laughed Mr. Prescott. "That was Tom Reade, and he was playing a trick on you---with our permission. Now he's being chased. Do you want to go out and aid that crowd in capturing him?"

"Of course I don't, sir," replied Dick, who knew full well that such a sturdy high school athlete as Tom Reade was in very little danger of being caught by any citizen runners to be found on the street at that time of night. "But what did Tom do, Dad?"

"I don't just know," admitted the bookseller. "Reade told us there would be a smash of glass, but that it would be harmless. He warned your mother, Dick, so that she wouldn't he startled when it came. Tom did the right thing in warning your mother. I wish all boys could realize that only cowards and fools go about frightening women."

"But something else happened," insisted Mrs. Prescott. "I wonder what it was?"

"Suppose we take a lantern and go out in the back yard and see," proposed Dick.

While Dick was finding the lantern the elder Prescott closed the front of the store, also drawing down the shades for the night.

Dick's mother followed him into the rear yard. The fragments of the bottle under one of the store windows told the whole story to one as experienced in jokes as Dick Prescott.

"But see how wet the ground is," Mrs. Prescott remarked after Dick had explained the trick.

"That was because I didn't recognize the joker, and emptied the contents of my water pitcher on him just as he broke the bottle," Dick smiled. "Poor old Tom. That was really a shame!"

"But why did you pour the water on him?" asked Mrs. Prescott.

"Because I felt sure that the prowler was up to some mischief, and I wanted to mark him for identification, mother," Dick explained. "If we had found a fellow on the street looking as though he had just come out of the river, we'd have known our man, wouldn't we? Poor Tom! I don't blame him for letting out that yell when that drenching splash hit him."

"I hope he didn't get caught by the men who started after him," sighed Mrs. Prescott.

"Don't worry about Tom, mother," urged Dick. "No one about here could catch him, unless he happened to be a member of the Gridley High School Eleven!"

But was it true that Tom Reade had escaped without disaster? That remained to be seen.

## CHAPTER II
## DODGE AND BAYLISS HEAR SOMETHING

I f we start to-morrow we must hustle all day long to-day," declared Dave Darrin.

"That's true," agreed Greg Holmes, as the two boys stood on a side street not far from Main Street in Gridley.

"I wish the rest of the fellows would hurry along," Dave went on impatiently.

"At all events, I wish Dick would hurry up, as he has charge of the arrangements," Greg made answer. "Oh, my! But I'm getting anxious to see the fish nibble."

"I thought you didn't care especially about fishing," Dave murmured, regarding his friend.

"Probably, as far as mere fishing goes, I don't care so very much," young Holmes assented. "But when fishing means weeks of outdoor life, free from the noise and dust of the town---then I'm simply wild about fishing as an excuse for getting away. Probably at the end of our fun we'll all be so sick of fish, from having had to eat so much of it, that any one of us will run away and hide when we suspect that the home folks are planning to send us on errands to a fish store. It would be all the same to me if we were going clamming, or hunting, or on any other kind of expedition, as long as it brought us to life under canvas and sleeping in the very place where pure, fresh air is made. Here comes Dick now!"

Young Prescott came swiftly up to his friends.

"Well, I think I've gotten about everything fixed," Dick announced.

"Tell us all the plans," urged Greg eagerly.

"What's the matter with waiting until all the other fellows show up?" Prescott inquired. "That will save me from having to go twice over the same ground. While we're waiting I'll tell you Tom Reade's latest one."

"A funny trick?" queried Greg.

"Needless question!" rebuked Dave Darrin. "Tell us about the latest one, Dick."

Thereupon the leader of Dick & Co. told of Tom's scheme for making people think one of their windows broken.

"Did it sound real?" Dave demanded.

"Did it?" inquired Dick. "It fooled me. I thought surely that our rear store window had been smashed to pieces. The sound is as natural as any joker could wish. But I haven't told you the other half of the story."

Thereupon Dick told about the pitcher of water dumped so unerringly on Tom, and of Reade's flight with the crowd pursuing him.

"I'd like to have been near enough to hear just what Tom said when the water struck him," laughed Darrin.

"Did the people running after him catch him?" asked Greg.

"I don't believe so," Dick Prescott smiled. "When Tom gets under way in earnest, his middle name, as you may have observed, is Double Speed---and then a bit more."

"Who's talking about me?" gruffly demanded Reade, coming up behind the group. "Dick, you old rascal! That was a mean trick you played upon me when you hurled that water down on me last night! But say, didn't it sound just like a three dollar pane of glass going to pieces?"

"It certainly did," laughed Prescott. "And by the way, Tom, did the water, when it struck, make you think at all about what you've read of Niagara Falls?"

"Hang you!" grumbled Tom, shaking a fist. "Why did you pour the wet stuff on me like that?"

"Because I was fooled myself," Dick promptly rejoined. "I thought some rascal was plotting mischief to the store. I wanted to mark that rascal with a suit of wet clothes, then run down in the street and collar him with his wet clothes on as a marker. But Dad called me back, and so I missed you. I heard the crowd after you, however. Did you get caught, Tom?"

Reade's answer was something of a growl.

"What happened between you and the crowd?" pressed Darrin, scenting some news from Reade's mysterious, half-sulky manner.

"Never you mind," Tom growled.

"Don't tell us," Dick urged. "We can guess a few things, anyway. You've a bruised spot over your left cheek bone that looks like the mark of a punch on the face."

"Go ahead and tell us what happened, Tom," urged Greg.

Reade only scowled.

"Anyway, you must have avenged yourself," Dick smiled. "Just look at the way the knuckles of your right hand are skinned. You certainly hit someone hard."

Tom flushed quickly as he glanced at the knuckles in question, then thrust his right hand into his pocket with an air of indifference.

"Be a good fellow and tell us the finish of the adventure," begged Darrin.

"Certainly," grinned Reade. "The end of my adventure was-----"

"Yes, yes!" pressed Greg, as Tom hesitated.

"The end of the adventure came," Tom continued maliciously, "when I turned out the gas in my little room and hopped into bed. I slept like a top, thank you."

"Now, now, now!" Dick warned him. "Thomas, you're hiding something from us!"

"If I am, it's my own business, and I've a right to hide it," retorted Tom, smiling once more, though still uncommunicative.

At this moment Hazelton and Dan Dalzell, otherwise known as Danny Grin, came up. They, too, had to hear all about the bottle-breaking trick.

"How did you ever come to think of a thing like that, Tom?" asked Harry Hazelton.

"I thought of it before I tried it out at Dick's," Reade rejoined, and explained how he had helped Timmy Finbrink out of a scrape.

"What did you say the fellow's name is, Tom?" Dick asked.

"His name is Timmy Finbrink," Reade rejoined, "and he looks the part. Just one glance at Timmy, and you know that he's all that the name implies."

Then followed, for the benefit of the two latest arrivals, the story of Tom's attempt in the rear of the Prescott bookstore.

Harry and Dalzell duly admired the bruise on Tom's face.

"Now, be a gentleman, Tom," urged Harry mischievously, "and let us have a good, satisfying look at your skinned knuckles."

"Umph!" grunted Reade.

"Or, at least," pursued Harry relentlessly, "tell us just what it was into which you ran to get such a mark on your face."

"Umph!" retorted Reade once more. "Danny, in the name of mercy, take that grin of yours around the corner and lose it!"

"I'll try," promised Dan, "provided you'll tell us who caught you last night, and why he punched your face."

But Tom, knowing that he had them all wild with curiosity, refused to reveal the secret.

"Now, let's get back to the big fishing trip," begged Greg Holmes. "Dick, what's the plan?"

"We start to-morrow," Prescott rejoined.

"Humph!" grunted Holmes. "We knew that all along. What we want are the particulars in detail."

"In the next place, then," Dick replied, "we shall devote a good deal of our time, while away, to the pleasurable excitement of fishing."

"Perhaps you won't be able to get away," Greg retorted, "if you go on stringing us in that fashion. I warn you that we're becoming impatient."

"That's right," nodded Dave Darrin. "Get down to actual particulars, Dick."

"Well, then," Prescott resumed, "we meet at the same old grocery store in the morning. There we stock up with food."

"Are we going to hire a horse and wagon for transporting our tent, cots, bedding and food?" Dan asked.

"No," Dick replied. "I've been thinking that over, and the funds won't stand it. So I've rented a push cart for two dollars. We can keep it as long as we need it. The tent, folding cots, blankets, pillows and kitchen utensils will go on the cart."

"Do we have to push that cart?" demanded Danny Grin, looking displeased.

"We do, if we want the cart to go along with us," Dick admitted.

Danny Grin groaned dismally as he remarked:

"That one detail of the arrangements just about spoils all the pleasure of the trip, then."

"No, it won't," Dick reported promptly. "I've looked into that. The wheels are well greased---the axles, I mean. I've loaded the cart with more weight than we shall put on it, and it pushes along very easily. If we come to a bad stretch of road, then two fellows can manage the cart at a time.  The scheme saves us a lot of expense, fellows."

"Will all the food go on the cart, tool" asked Dave.

"Each one of us can carry some of the food," Dick replied.

Then his eye, roving from face to face, took in the fact that his chums were not impressed with the proposed method of transportation.

"Cheer up, fellows," he begged.  "You'll find that it will be pretty easy, after all."

"I'd rather believe you, Dick, than have it proved to me," was Tom Reade's dejected answer.  "I thought we were going away for pleasure and rest, but I suppose we can work our way if we have to."

None of these high school boys are strangers to our readers. Everyone remembers the first really public appearance of Dick & Co., as set forth in the first volume of the "*Grammar School Boys Series*."  Then we met them again in the first volume of the "*High School Boys Series*," entitled, "*The High School Freshmen*." That stormy first year of high school life was one that Dick & Co. could never forget.  In the second volume, "*The High School Pitcher*," we found Dick & Co. actively engaged in athletics, though in their sophomore year they did not attempt to make the eleven, but waited until the spring to try for the baseball nine. In the third volume, "*The High School Left End*," Dick & Co. were shown in their struggles to make the eleven, against some clever candidates, and also in the face of bitter opposition from a certain clique of high school boys who considered themselves to be of better social standing than Dick and his chosen comrades.

In the "*High School Boys' Vacation Series*" our readers have followed Dick & Co. through their summer pleasures and sports. In the first volume of this present series, "*The High School Boys' Canoe Club*," the adventures are described that fell to the lot of Prescott, Darrin, Reade and the others in the summer following their freshman high school year.  In the second volume, "*The High School Boys In Summer Camp*," our readers found an absorbing narrative of the startling doings of Dick & Co. in the summer following their sophomore year.  And now, in this present volume, we at last come upon our young friends at the beginning of their vacation season after the completion of their junior year, with its football victories. Now they are budding seniors, ready to enter the final, graduating class of Gridley

High School in the coming autumn.

As Dick looked into the faces of his chums he laughed.

"So you don't like the push-cart idea, eh?" he demanded. "All right; if you fellows would rather loaf than eat-----"

"We can hire a horse, and still have money enough left to eat," protested Tom. "See here, Dick, although fishing is great fun while it lasts, we shan't be out all summer on a fishing trip. We don't need such a lot of money for, say, only a two or three weeks' trip."

"Yes; I think two or three weeks will see us in from our fishing trip," Prescott admitted. "But if we do come back early, fellows, then we shall need some other kind of a trip for August, won't we?"

"Say, that's right!" cried Dave Darrin, his eyes glistening. "Fellows, we are troubled with wooden heads. While we've been thinking of nothing but a fishing trip in July, Dick has actually had the brains to figure out that we might like to go away on some other kind of outing in August."

"Such an idea did occur to me," replied Dick.

"What's the scheme for August, Dick?" demanded Greg eagerly.

"Out with it!" insisted Hazelton.

Dick shook his head.

"Now, don't be mean," insisted Danny Grin. "Dick, you owe it to us, almost, to let us get a little look at the machinery that's moving in the back of your head."

"I haven't an August plan---at least, not one that is clear enough for me to submit it and put it to vote before you," Dick went on. "Fellows, let's set about this present fishing trip, for this month, and then, while we're away, talk up the proper scheme for August. Whatever we do in the way of fun, next month, will be sure to be better planned if we wait a little before talking it over."

"All right, then," agreed Tom Reade with a sigh. "But I warn you, Dick, and all you fellows, that if Prescott is too stingy with news about his August plan, I shall put forth one of my own."

"What's your August plan, Tom?" demanded Greg.

"I'm not going to tell you---yet," Reade rejoined, shaking his head mysteriously.

"There are a lot of things that you're not telling us," Dave reminded him. "Just for one little thing, you're not telling us what happened to you last night after you let a lot of strange men chase you out of Dick's street."

"They didn't chase me off the street!" declared Tom indignantly.

"Then what did happen?" quizzed Danny Grin.

"They all tried to beat me in a foot race," Tom declared, "and I put it all over them!"

"Yet someone must have passed you, or got in front of you," teased Greg. "Look at the bruise on your face, and your knuckles."

"Oh, that happened when-----" began Tom, then paused abruptly.

"Yes, yes," pressed Danny Grin. "Tell us about it."

"All right," agreed Tom, "I will. You see, when I got home and into bed, I had a sort of nightmare. Just suppose, for instance, that the mark on my face is where the nightmare kicked me and that I skinned my knuckles against the bedstead when I tried to jump over the bed to return the nightmare's kick."

"Tom Reade," called Dave sternly, "hold up your right hand!"

"Look out, Darry! You're not going to ask Tom to swear to the truth of a yarn like that, are you?" asked Dick anxiously.

"You may let your hand down again, young man," decided Dave, and Tom, as his hand reached his side, heaved a sigh expressive of great relief.

"Now, have you fellows got your tackle all ready?" Dick went on. "Remember the different things in the way of tackle that each of us was to bring."

The others assured their leader that the matter of tackle had been attended to.

"Then your bedding and your clothing are the only other matters to be considered," Dick went on, "as we're to travel light."

"As we don't take a horse along," suggested Tom, "then I take it that we are not going to carry any planking for a tent floor."

"We can't very well do that," Dick answered him. "Fellows, the real thing for us to do, on this trip, is to learn how to move fast and light. We must learn how to do without many things and yet have just as good a time."

"I think that's good sense," murmured Dave. "At the same time, I'll admit, at first blush, that I don't care particularly for the motion of the push cart. That means a lot of extra work for us, if we change camping sites often."

"Then let's put it to a vote whether to hire a horse and wagon, and give up the idea of an August trip," proposed Dick.

"No need whatever of taking any vote," broke in Tom. "All of us want that August trip, too, and we know that we haven't purses as big as a bank's vault."

And that opinion prevailed, without dissent.

"Greg's house ought to be the best place to keep the push cart over night," Dick continued. "I'll have the cart there at four this afternoon. Suppose you fellows meet us there, with your bedding and clothing for the trip?"

This also was agreed upon.

While the boys stood there chatting not one of them suspected how eagerly they were being watched by two pairs of eyes.

On the same side of the street, only a door below them, was an unrented cottage. One of the windows of this cottage, upstairs, was open, though closed blinds concealed the fact. Between these blinds peered two young men.

That cottage was the property of Mr. Dodge, vice-president of one of Gridley's banks.

Readers of "*The High School Left End*" have good reason to remember the banker's son, Bert Dodge. He and his friend, Bayliss, also the scion of a wealthy family, had been members of the notorious "sorehead" group in the last year's football squad at Gridley High School.

As our readers well remember, Dodge and Bayliss had carried their opposition to Dick & Co. to such dishonorable extent that they had been given the "silence" by the boys and girls attending the Gridley High School.

Dodge and Bayliss had thereupon left home to attend a private school, and they had gone away from Gridley with bitter hatred of Dick & Co. rankling in their hearts.

Just at this present moment Dodge and Bayliss were back in the home town. Deeply and properly humiliated by the contempt with which they were regarded in Gridley, these two "soreheads" had concealed from all but members of their families the fact that they were in town.

Bert had secured from his father the keys of the cottage. Two cots had been placed in a front room. Late the night before Dodge had brought food supplies to the cottage. Here the two youngsters were to remain secretly for a few days until Bayliss received from his family, then abroad, the money needed for his summer outing. What the elder Dodge did not know or even suspect, was that his son and Bayliss had returned with some half-formed plans of paying back old scores against Dick & Co.

"I knew this cottage was the place for us," Bert whispered. "As I told you, Bayliss, this corner is a favorite meeting place for Prescott and his fellow muckers."

"From what I hear, they're going to leave town for a few weeks," replied Bayliss.

"Yes; going out into the wilds on some sort of fishing jaunt."

"I wish we knew their plans better than we do," murmured Bayliss.

"Don't believe they know 'em themselves any too well," sneered Bert Dodge. "However, we don't need to know where they're going. We can follow 'em, can't we?"

"Yes; and get jolly well thumped for our pains, maybe," retorted Bayliss dryly.

"Well, if you're afraid, we'll let 'em depart in peace," mocked Bert.

"Who's afraid?" demanded Bayliss irritably.

"I hope you're not," retorted Bert Dodge.

"If you're not afraid---if you're as thoroughly game as I am---then we'll have some satisfaction out of those fellows."

"Lead me to it!" ordered Bayliss hotly.

"I will, to-morrow morning," promised Bert Dodge. "If you stick to me, we'll make those muckers sorry they ever knew us!"

"We must be under way by nine o'clock," the listeners heard Dick say. "We go west, over Main Street. We must start promptly, for we have sixteen miles to go to our first camp at the second lake in the Cheney Forest."

"Do you hear that?" whispered Bert. "The idiots have given us their full route! We can leave at four in the morning, and won't have to follow 'em at all. We can be there ahead of time, and have all the lines laid."

"Somehow," sounded Dave Darrin's voice, "I have a hunch, fellows, that we're going to have the finest time we ever had in our lives."

"We would have," sighed Tom Reade, "if it weren't for that push cart."

"At four o'clock this afternoon, then, and be prompt," called Dick, preparing to leave the others.

"Wait a moment," urged Dave.

"What's the matter?" inquired Dick, halting.

"Tom's just on the point of telling us what really happened to him last night," smiled Darry.

"Humph!" grunted Reade, walking briskly away.

"I can tell what's going to happen to 'em all on some other nights," whispered Bert Dodge in his friend's ear.

"To get square with those muckers, who drove us out of Gridley High School and out of town is my only excuse for living at present," sniffed Bayliss.

## CHAPTER III
## DICK & CO. DRIVEN UP A TREE

D ick!"

"Yes?" replied Prescott, turning and looking back at Tom, whose turn it now was to furnish motive power to the loaded cart.

"How far did you say it was from Gridley to the second lake?" asked Reade.

"Sixteen miles."

"I've pushed the cart more than that far already," grunted Tom. "I'm willing to wager that the lake is more than a hundred and twenty miles from Gridley."

"Suppose it is," scoffed Dave, falling back beside the cart "Tom, just think of the fine training your back muscles are getting out of this work!"

"I'll tell you all about that, Darry," grumbled Reade, "when you've had your turn for ten minutes. How much longer does my turn run, Dick?"

"Five minutes," replied Prescott, after glancing at his watch. "Are you going to be able to hold out that long?"

"Yes; if I live that long," sighed Tom.

Dick and Hazelton had each taken their fifteen minute turns at pushing the cart. The boys had already put some distance between themselves and Gridley. Dick & Co. were tramping down a well-shaded road bounded by prosperous-looking farms. Two miles further on the boys would branch off through a long stretch of woods where the road was rougher. Here two youngsters would be needed for the work, one pushing, while the other hauled on a rope made fast to the front of the cart.

Five of the boys were well laden with miscellaneous packages of food. Tom, on account of pushing the cart, had been permitted to place his load on the already well-packed cart.

"Time's up," called Dick. "Dave to the bat."

Smiling, Darry packed his own parcels in the cart.

"Whew! But it's good to get away from that thing," grunted Reade, mopping his forehead, as he stalked on ahead.

"Here, you, Tom!" called Danny Grin. "Take your personal pack off the cart and tote it like the rest of us."

Reade turned a comically scowling face to Dalzell.

"Danny," he demanded rebukingly, "why couldn't you hold your tongue?"

"Because, when I'm working hard, I don't like to see you shirk," replied Dalzell with a complacent grin.

"But consider Darry," urged Reade. "Note how strong, lithe and supple he is. Boy, he is much better fitted for pushing my personal pack on the cart than I am for carrying it."

"Stick a pin in the chat, Tom," advised Darrin briefly, "and take your truck off the cart. I want to begin enjoying myself."

"I'd carry twice as much as I have to, just for the sheer joy of hearing you kick like a Texas maverick by the time you've had the cart handles for two minutes," laughed Tom, as he took his own parcels off the cart. "Now, David, little giant, let us see you buckle down to your task---like a real or imitation man!"

Darry braced himself, gave a hitch, then started forward briskly.

"Get out of the way, you loiterers!" called Dave, overtaking Tom and Greg and shoving the front end of the cart against them. "Don't block the road!"

"That's what comes of hitching an express engine to a freight load," grunted Reade, as he made for the side of the road, brushing his clothes.

There was bound to be a lot of "kicking" over the work of handling the push cart, but Dick & Co. were in high spirits this hot July morning.

Weeks before, when first planning this trip, all had begun to "save up" toward outfits of khaki, leggings and all, and blue flannel shirts. These khaki clothes made the most serviceable of all camping costumes.

"I begin to feel like a soldier," laughed Dick contentedly.

"So do I," agreed Tom Reade. "I feel like a poor dub of a soldier who has been sent to march across a continent on the line of the equator. I believe eggs would cook in any of my pockets!"

"Cut out all the grumbling and the discomfort talk," warned Dave Darrin.

"Well, I don't know that I need to grumble, if you can feel contented behind that old cart," laughed Reade. "How does it go, Darry?"

"I haven't begun to notice, as yet," replied Dave coolly.

Tom eyed him suspiciously.

"Darry," he remarked presently, "you're talented."

"In what way?" Dave inquired.

"You're one of the most talented fibbers I ever encountered. You've been pushing that cart all of four minutes, and you pretend that you don't notice the work."

"I expected to work when I left home," Darrin informed him. "If I hadn't felt that I could endure a little fatigue, then I'd have remained at home and looked for a job sleeping in a mattress factory's show-room."

Tom subsided after that. Dave's fifteen minutes were up presently, but he declined to accept relief at the push cart until they reached the point where their road branched off on to the rougher highway. Now, Greg and Hazelton took the cart, Greg at the handles, Hazelton pulling ahead on the rope.

Thus they went along, for some five minutes, when Dick, who was in the lead, reached a small covered bridge over a noisy, rushing creek.

Just as Dick gained the entrance to the bridge his gaze fell upon a large white sheet of paper tacked there. The word "Notice," written in printing characters, stared him in the face.

Dick read, then called back quietly:

"Halt! Here's something we've got to look into at once."

The cart handlers willingly enough dropped their burden. All hands crowded forward to read what was written underneath on the sheet of paper. It ran thus:

"All passers-by are cautioned that a mad dog, frothing at the mouth, has passed this way, going west. Officers have gone in pursuit of the animal, but passers-by may encounter the dog before the officers do. The dog is a huge English mastiff, without collar. Turn back unless armed!"

"Fine and cheery!" exclaimed Tom Reade, looking rather startled despite his light comment.

"And, just as it happens, this is the only road in the country that we want to use just at present," commented Dick Prescott.

"Shall we go ahead, keeping a sharp lookout?" asked Dave.

"I don't know," Dick muttered. "We'll have to think that over a bit."

"There are six of us, and we can cut good, stout clubs before we proceed farther," suggested Greg Holmes.

"Yes, and probably, if attacked, we could finish the dog," Dick went on. "Yet, most likely, before we did kill the brute, he'd have bitten at least one of us."

"I'll go on, if the rest of you fellows want to," observed Danny Grin. "At the same time, it looks like taking a big chance, doesn't it?"

"It's taking a chance, of course," Dick admitted. "The dog may be running yet, and we might never get within ten, or even twenty, miles of him. Or, the officers may have caught and killed the brute by this time. Or, the mastiff might bound at us from the woods at any moment now."

"Whether we go back or keep on, we're fairly likely to meet the mad dog," suggested Tom. "Mr. Chairman, I rise to move, sir, that we cut clubs at once, and do the rest of our talking afterwards!"

"The motion is seconded and carried," called Dick, darting into the woods. "Come on and find the clubs."

Less than forty seconds afterwards each of the six boys was cutting a stout sapling, which he forthwith trimmed.

"I believe I could kill anything but an ox with this," observed Reade, eyeing his bludgeon.

"Look out!" called Danny Grin, as if in alarm.

In a twinkling Tom dropped his club, dashed at a young oak tree and began to climb, thinking that the dog had suddenly appeared.

"Stop that nonsense, Dan---and everyone of you!" called Dick sharply. "Let no one knowingly give any false alarms, or we might disregard a real warning when it comes."

Tom sheepishly dropped to the ground, picked up his cudgel, then gazed at Dalzell with a look that had "daggers" in it.

"I'll owe you one for that, Danny Grin," Reade remarked, "and I'm always careful about paying my debts."

"Now that we have our clubs," suggested Dick, "let's get back to the road and discuss what we're going to do."

"Surely," hinted Dave, "we can find some other road and keep on our way."

"Undoubtedly," Greg nodded. "But the mad dog might cross through the woods and be found waiting for us on that other road. Or, he may now be headed for the second lake, or even be there now."

"Let's vote on what we're going to do," urged Hazelton. "Dick, what do you say?"

"I don't know what to say," their young leader answered. "I don't like to see our party cheated out of our vacation. Neither do I care to take too many chances of having our vacation changed into a tragedy. I've never had hydrophobia, but I've a strong notion that it wouldn't be pleasant. I know just how you fellows feel. You hate to lose your fun."

"We do hate to lose our fun," agreed Darry.

"And yet you don't want to have an encounter with a dog that has hydrophobia."

"We don't," approved Tom Reade. "Dick, you have a truly wonderful intellect when it comes to successful guessing."

"There's a cloud of dust up the road to the west," discovered Greg Holmes.

In an instant all eyes were turned that way.

"Can that be the dog?" asked Darry. "Something is traveling this way and stirring up a lot of dust."

Whatever the moving object was, it appeared to be half a mile away up the straight, dust-covered road.

"Until we find out what it is," Dick suggested, "I believe that tree climbing will prove healthful exercise."

Quickly they moved the push cart a little to one side of the road. Then they ran for trees, but every member of Dick & Co. retained his hold on his bludgeon.

The dust cloud was coming nearer. From the elevation of his perch in a tree Dick soon discovered and announced:

"It's a horse and wagon coming this way."

"Maybe it's the officers returning from the hunt," suggested Reade, who was on a lower limb of the next tree.

"There's only one man in the wagon, and he's whipping up the horse," Dick announced.

"There are good enough reasons for the man wanting his horse to hurry," chuckled Danny.

"Maybe the dog is in pursuit now," hinted Darrin.

Dick, who had the best view of the road to the westward, peered carefully.

"I don't see anything to suggest a pursuing dog," Prescott made answer. "If the dog is near, he must be running under the trees along the side of the road."

Greg climbed up beside his leader.

"Why, that man has stopped whipping the horse," young Holmes declared. "And is lighting his pipe. That doesn't look as though he were very much scared about anything."

"We'll stay where we are until we've talked with the man," Dick decided.

Just before reaching the other end of the covered bridge the driver, a farmer, and with what looked like a light load of farm produce in the body of the wagon, slowed his horse down to a walk, at which gait he drove over the bridge. Then, sighting the boys up in the trees, and each with a club, he reined up.

"Hello, boys!" he called drawlingly. "Who's been a-chasing you? What scared you?"

"Read that notice, sir, tacked up at the bridge entrance," urged Dick.

Alighting, and drawing a pair of spectacles from a vest pocket, the farmer complied.

"Mad dog, eh?" he drawled. "Sho!"

"Did you see anything of the brute?" called Darry.

"No; I didn't," answered the farmer. "Don't believe there is any mad dog along the way, either. I've reined up and talked with neighbors during the last hour and a half along the way. They didn't mention nothin' 'bout any peevish dogs. Now, it stands to reason that the officers would have stopped and warned folks along the road, don't it? And the neighbors would have passed the gossip with me, wouldn't they?"

"Didn't you see any officers coming from this way?" asked Dick.

"Nary one," rejoined the farmer. "Only fellers that passed me, coming from this direction, was two young dudes---I sh'd say about your ages. They was in a high-toned speed wagon-----"

"Automobile?" asked Reade.

"Said so, didn't I?" drawled the farmer. "Them dudes looked mighty tickled about something. They was laughin' a whole lot and looked mighty well pleased with themselves. Do you reckon they was any friends of your'n, trying to have fun with you?"

"I can't recall any friends who would try to put up such a pleasant surprise for us," said Dick dryly, as he slipped down to the ground. "What did the fellows in the automobile look like, sir?"

That farmer possessed well-developed powers of observation, as was proved by the minute descriptions he gave of the two young men.

Dick's chums, who had now joined him at the roadside, looked puzzled. Then light dawned in Tom's eyes.

"Jupiter!" cried Reade. "If it weren't that they're not in this part of the country, I'd say that the pair were Dodge and Bayliss!"

"How do you know they're not in this part of the country?" asked Prescott dryly. Then, of the farmer, he further inquired:

"What kind of a car were they driving, sir?"

"A red Smattach, last year's model," answered the man.

"That's just what the Dodge automobile runabout is, and Smattach cars are not common in this section," muttered Prescott. Then he went over to take a keener look at the written notice on the sheet of white paper.

"This looks like disguised handwriting; it's backhanded," Dick mused aloud. "But I notice one thing peculiar. Who makes a funny little quirl at the beginning of a letter 'm,' such as you see in this writing?"

"Bert Dodge!" flashed Dave Darrin, an indignant light flashing in his eyes. "So we're six simpletons, held up by his shady tricks, are we? If Bert Dodge is anywhere ahead of us on the road, then I hope we have the good luck to meet him under conditions where he can't jam on the speed and get away from us!"

"Joke on you all, is it?" asked the farmer, grinning quizzically.

"It looks like it," admitted Dick sheepishly. "You're sure that none of the folks west of here heard anything of a mad dog, are you?"

"Pretty sure," nodded the farmer.

"Then this notice isn't really needed up here," replied Dick, carefully pulling the tacks, after which he folded the paper and tucked it in one of his pockets. "We're mightily obliged to you, sir."

"Oh, you're welcome," grinned the farmer, as he gathered up the reins over his horse. "I've got to be getting along. I'm late in Gridley now."

"If that man is too talkative in Gridley, folks will hear how we got sold," yawned Tom, gazing after the farm wagon. "Then---my! Won't folks be laughing at us?"

"It's a mean trick," cried Dave indignantly. "I wish I had that Dodge fellow here, right now! I believe that I'm master of enough English to convey to him an idea of just what I think of him!"

"I wouldn't waste any of my carefully acquired English on him," growled Tom Reade.

"What would you do---skin your other knuckles?" inquired Danny Grin innocently.

"We're wasting too much time punishing a fellow who isn't here," Dick broke in. "Let's get forward. After another mile Dalzell and I will take the cart and get it over some of the ground. Now, forward, march!"

It was noticed that Dave Darrin walked with clenched-fists. Tom took long strides that carried him in advance of the others. Dick Prescott was mostly silent, yet in his eyes there was a steady light, and a grim look about his mouth, that bespoke the possibility of some inconvenience to Bert Dodge and his friend, should that pair fall into the hands of Dick & Co. within the next hour.

At noon Dick & Co. halted. Under the shade of a group of trees, close to a roadside spring, they built two small fires. Over one they made coffee; over the other, they fried bacon and eggs. This, with bread, constituted the meal. A brief rest, then on they went once more.

It was toward five o'clock when Dick and Tom, who knew the road from having tramped over it before, announced that they were less than half a mile from the point where they would turn in to go to the second lake.

At this time Greg and Dan were managing the push cart. Tom and Dick strode on ahead, watching for the first sign of the path that should lead down to their intended camp site.

Suddenly, however, Prescott seized Reade by the arm, halting him.

"What's the matter?" asked Tom.

"Sh!---" Dick piloted his friend in behind a line of bushes, then went cautiously ahead.

"Look over there!" whispered Dick.

Tom Reade gave a start when he found himself gazing at a red runabout that stood just off the road and apparently deserted.

"Humph! That's a Smattach, too," declared Tom. "It must be the Dodge car. Bert and Bayliss must be somewhere about."

Dick stood surveying the car with speculative eyes.

"I know what you're thinking about," Tom whispered. "Wait; I'll go back and halt the fellows and bring Dave forward with me."

In a few moments this had been done. Darry gazed at the red Smattach with gleaming eyes.

"This is surely our chance!" he muttered. "Now, what can we do?"

All three were silent for a few moments. Then Tom Reade smote his thigh with one hand.

"I have it," he muttered excitedly.

"Then don't be stingy with your secret," urged Dave. "Out with at least a part of it."

For some moments Dick, Dave and Tom remained engaged in a rapid interchange of whispers, all the time glancing about them.

## CHAPTER IV
## STALLING THE RED "SMATTACH"

That's the very thing!" muttered Tom Reade at last.

"It can't get us into any scrape with the law, can it?" queried Dave Darrin, with almost unwonted caution.

"I don't see how it can," smiled Dick Prescott. "I'm no lawyer, but I can't see how our trick, the way we intend to play it, can be called a breach of the law."

"Let's not lose any time with the game," urged Reade. "Let's get in and do it before Dodge and Bayliss come back. I wonder where they are, anyway?"

"I don't care where they are," said Dave, "as long as they keep away from here until we're through with what we intend to do."

From its place in the runabout car Tom drew forth a wheel-jack. This he and Dave fitted under an axle, raising the wheel half aft inch off the ground. Dick rapidly remove the tire from that front wheel.

By the time he had finished Tom ran with the jack around to the other front wheel, removing the tire from it also.

As the red runabout carried no extra tires the little car was now hopelessly stalled until relief was brought to the scene.

"Now, I'll slip back and bring the fellows on," Dick whispered. "Tom, you take Dave down to the camp site. I'll be right along with the other fellows."

Tom and Dave started along the forest path, each carrying a tire slung over one shoulder.

Dick, darting back, brought up the other fellows. All took a gleeful look at the red Smattach as they passed, then hurried on.

Down to a level bit of ground at the lakeside Dick led the last of his friends. Tom and Dave were already there, the two pneumatic tires standing against the trunk o a tree.

Dick's first move was to take a rope from the cart. This, after being passed through the rubber tires, was tied between two trees, clothesline fashion.

"Now, let's rustle all the stuff off the cart," urged Dick. "Be quick about it. We want the tent up in good shape before darkness falls."

It is not much of a trick to raise a tent twelve feet by twenty, when there are six pairs of hands to do it. The two centre poles were adjusted to the ridge-pole, and all three were pushed in under the canvas.

"Up with her," called Dick.

As the tent was raised, Tom and Greg were left holding the centre poles in place. With a sledge Dick drove a corner stake, and a guy-rope was made fast to it. One after another the remaining corner stakes were quickly driven and the ropes made fast. The tent would now stand by itself.

Dick and Dave, Tom and Greg now attended to two stakes at a time, making the other guy-ropes fast.

"Danny, you may set in all the wall-pegs," said Dick, standing back to survey the really neat job.

"I've been thinking-----" began Dalzell.

"Then let Hazelton do the wall-pegging," retorted Dick tersely.

"I've been thinking-----" Dalzell went on, "that it would be awfully funny, wouldn't it, if that red Smattach belonged, not to Dodge, but to some fellow we've never seen before?"

"It would be inexpressibly funny!" growled Tom Reade. "And what would be funnier than anything else would be our frantic efforts to make a satisfactory explanation."

"We could be arrested for theft, couldn't we?" asked Greg, glancing up apprehensively from the side wall pegging.

"Hardly that," replied Dick, with a shake of his head. "Theft, as I understand it, usually carries with it the sale of the plunder, or its concealment. We have hung up the tires where anyone who is interested may see them. Still, it would be awkward making explanations to strangers, and we'd all feel mighty cheap."

"Then maybe we'll have our chance to feel that way," suggested Danny Grin, his mouth opening still wider.

"Don't waste your time on pleasant thoughts, like that," grunted Reade. "Try to think of something sad."

"If it's the Dodge car, could Bert make any trouble for us?" Darrin wanted to know.

"Hardly," answered young Prescott. "We've simply played a clever trick on Dodge and Bayliss. As our excuse we could point out a trick they palmed off on us earlier in the day. We'd be quits. You needn't fear Dodge. Never, since that time when he got so awfully beaten over the assault charge he made against me, has he felt that he wanted to face me in court again."

"You fellows wait here, and don't be worried if I don't come back soon," interposed Darry suddenly.

"What are you going to do?" demanded Tom Reade.

But Dave had slipped away. When he chose to be as mysterious as that, Dick Prescott knew better than to question his chum.

Rapidly the work of straightening camp proceeded. Dave was back in a little more than half an hour. Yet he returned so noiselessly that he was in camp before the others realized his presence.

"Well-----?" asked Dick eagerly.

"Come into the tent, fellows," whispered Dave.

When Darrin had them inside he went on, in a low voice:

"It's the Dodge car, all right. I hid behind a tree nearby the car and waited until they returned. When they found the front tires missing they were furious. Bayliss said we fellows had done it, but Bert said he didn't believe we were anywhere near here as yet. I slipped away and left them arguing. Dodge wants Bayliss to walk to the nearest place where he can telephone to a garage to send a man out with new tires. Bayliss says it's the Dodge car, and Bert can do the walking. It looks as though they would come to blows, and, as I've been gently reared, with a distaste for fighting, I slipped away."

"If they want to come down and look along the edge of this lake, they'll soon find out where their tires are," Dick Prescott chuckled. "But they'll have to come right in here to camp and ask for their property."

"Which they won't greatly care about doing," laughed Reade.

"Let them stay away until their nerves improve, then," said Dick briefly. "Now, let's see; we've got to set up the cots and bedding, and get the two lanterns filled and trimmed for the evening. That ought not to take many minutes."

Nor did it. When this had been done, Dick asked:

"Fellows, you know what we came here to do? Fish wouldn't taste bad for supper, would it? Which two of you want to go and try your luck for perch? They'll bite, even after dark."

Tom and Hazelton made a hasty selection of tackle, also producing a can of bait that had been brought along from Gridley.

Then Tom and Harry disappeared, taking with them one of the lanterns. A quarter of a mile below the camp were the ruins of an old pier from which they could cast their lines.

Where the perch are plentiful there is little skill involved in such fishing. Perch will bite after dark. The hook is baited and dropped in. The fish take hold greedily, rarely falling from the hook afterward.

While Tom and Harry were still fishing darkness fell. The two Gridley boys fished on in silence, adding frequently to the two crotched stick "strings" that flopped on the end of the pier.

"We've thirty-nine perch. That's enough, even for a hungry crowd like ours," said Tom at last, after lighting the lantern.

"Here is the fortieth, then," called Hazelton, as he felt a tug at his line. He landed a pound perch almost under Tom's nose.

"Good enough business, this," declared Tom contentedly. "I hope the fellows have everything else ready."

Tom carried the lantern; each boy carried a string of fish. As they neared camp, Danny Grin espied them, and ran forward to see the size of the catch.

"Here they are!" called Dalzell. "They've fish enough to feed a fat men's boarding house!"

"Bring them here," called Dick from a board beside which he and Greg crouched, each with a knife in hand.

One after another the fish were scaled and cleaned with a speed known only to old campers. Dave had two frying pans hot over a fire. In went the perch, sputtering in the fat and giving forth appetizing odors.

"My, but they're going to taste good!" declared Danny Grin.

Leaving Greg to finish with the cleaning of the fish Dick passed to another campfire, throwing into a hot pan the material for fried potatoes.

Ere long the meal was on the table---two boards placed across the tops of two boxes. It was a low table, but it served the purpose.

"My, but this fish tastes good!" murmured Tom Reade, as he picked a piece of fried perch free of the backbone and began eating it.

"We'll all of us find it the best meal ever, just because we've tramped far enough and worked hard enough to make any kind of decent food taste great," Dick smiled.

The supper over, and one of the campfires replenished, all six of the youngsters took the dishes down to the lake, carrying along two kettles of hot water, where a general dish-washing ensued. With so many to do the work, the camp was spick and span within twenty minutes.

"Now, I'm going to enjoy one thing that I haven't had all day, and that's some real rest," Prescott declared, throwing himself down upon the grass. "I don't believe I shall move until bedtime."

But he did. Already trouble was hovering over the camp. From out of the darkness beyond three pairs of eyes studied the campers in silence. One pair belonged to Bert Dodge, another the young Bayliss, and the third to a man of about middle age.

Dodge and Bayliss were thoroughly angry.

## CHAPTER V
## BERT DODGE HEARS THE BATTLE CRY

Ten minutes after Dick had thrown himself on the grass a rustling was heard above the camp. Then down the slope strode three figures.

Dick sat up, regarding the visitors in silence until they came within the fringe of the light of the campfire.

"Hello, Dodge," was Prescott's ready greeting. "I didn't hear you knock."

"Then maybe you will, before long," retorted Bert, in a voice of barely suppressed fury. "Prescott, you sneak, how long since you have added grand larceny to your other bad habits?"

"Try that over again," requested Dick calmly. "I don't believe I quite catch you."

"Yes, you do," Dodge retorted. "Come now, no lying about it."

"The nearest that I come to understanding you, as yet," Dick answered in an unruffled voice, "is that you appear to be trying to be offensive."

"I'll be more than offensive with you, before I get through!" cried Bert, his temper rising.

The third member of the visiting party was a man of about forty years, of sandy complexion and with a stubby, bristling red moustache. He looked like a man who had been born a fighter, though his face expressed keen attention rather than a desire to be quarrelsome. In dress this man looked as though he might be a farmer. Dick and his friends judged the man to be a rustic constable.

"A nice trick you played on us!" Bert went on angrily. "You took our front tires off the wheels of the car and ran away with them."

"Easy! Careful!" Dick smilingly advised. "Did anyone see us take the tires off and run away with them?"

Bert looked astonished, then gulped chokingly. Did Prescott and his friends intend to deny the charge?

"No one had to see you take the tires," Bert went on angrily. "All that is necessary is for us to discover the merchandise on you!"

"Then you have missed some tires, and you think I'm wearing them?" Dick chuckled.

"Don't try to sneak, lie or equivocate" commanded Bert Dodge, his face flushing with anger. "Those are my tires hanging from that line!"

"Are they?" Prescott inquired, in a tone of the mildest curiosity.

"You know they are!"

"Then, if the tires are your property, just help yourself!" Dick coolly answered. "If they are your tires, I will even offer to forego making any storage charges for the time they have been. hanging there."

"Hang you!" choked Bert

Then he turned to the man with them, demanding:

"Don't you see a pretty clear case of grand larceny here?"

"I can't sa-ay that I do---yet," drawled the stranger.

"You'll never see a clearer case!" quivered young Dodge.

To this the stranger did not reply. He had been looking over this sextette of high school boys, and if one might judge from his face, the man seemed to be rather favorably impressed by Dick & Co.

"If these are your tires," Dick went on smoothly, "would you mind removing them from our camp?"

"I won't," Bert answered hotly. "You fellows, who stole the tires, will take them back to the car from which you stole them, and there you will put the tires on again."

"You've missed some part of the idea in your haste," declared young Prescott.

"What do you mean?" gasped Dodge.

"I mean simply that we'll have nothing whatever to do with taking back the tires, or putting them on your wheels."

"Then I'll see what I can do to punish you all!" flared Bert hotly. "You're none of you any better than a lot of low-lived thieves!"

The situation was growing too warm for Dave Darrin, though Dick was still smiling.

Darry jumped to his feet, advancing upon Bert Dodge, who retreated a couple of steps.

"Dodge," Dave began, "you want to put a halter on your tongue. You can't come here to this camp and call too many names. You don't amount to much, of course, and nothing that you know how to say should be treated very seriously. It would be hard for a rascal like yourself to be really insulting to anyone possessed of the average degree of honor. But we came up here for pleasure and rest. Both your face and your voice---not particularly your words---are disturbing. If those are your tires, kindly take them and get out of camp!"

"You fellows will carry the tires back to the road, and you'll put them on the wheels," retorted Dodge hoarsely.

"As Dick has already told you, we'll do nothing of the sort," Dave flashed back at him. "All we want, Dodge, is for you to get out of this camp. Incidentally, if you want the tires, we shall offer no objections to your taking them with you."

"What have you to say to that?" demanded Bert hotly, turning to the man with the stubby red mustache.

"It seems to me like good judgment," replied the stranger.

"You say that?" screamed Bert, going into a blind passion. "Is that what we brought you here for?"

"I don't really know what you did bring me here for," replied the stranger. "All I know is that you stopped me, when I was driving past with my load of produce for the Gridley markets, and you offered me two dollars to come down here and not say much unless I was spoken to. I didn't come until you paid me the money. It was good pay, and I'll stay here an hour longer if you really think I owe you that much time."

"You're not a constable, or a sheriff's officer, are you, sir?" asked Dick pleasantly.

"Not unless someone made me one when I wasn't looking," replied the stranger, with a shrewd smile.

"I understand," nodded Prescott. "This fellow Dodge hired you to come down with him for more than one reason. In the first place, he and Bayliss were afraid to come here without backing. For another thing, Dodge thought that we'd guess you to be a constable, and I'll admit that I did mistake you for an officer at the outset. Dodge thought your presence would frighten us. You look like a decent man, sir, and I'm sorry to see you in such company. These two fellows were chased out of the Gridley High School just because they were considered unfit to associate with the members of the student body."

"That's a lie!" sputtered young Dodge.

"If you want to find out, sir, whether I'm speaking the truth," Dick went on, looking at the stranger, "just ask any well-informed citizen of Gridley whether Bert Dodge and his chum, Bayliss, were really chased out of the Gridley High School. You'll soon discover who the liar is---Dodge or myself."

"Hang you!" roared Bert, advancing with fists clenched. "I'll punch your head off your shoulders!"

"Wait one moment, though," advised the stranger, stepping between Dick and Bert. "Here, young man!"

"What's this?" Bert demanded, as the stranger forced something into one of his hands.

"It's the two-dollar bill you handed me," replied he of the stubby moustache. "I reckon that I made a mistake in taking it."

"Aren't you on my side any longer?" gasped Bert, in utter astonishment.

"I reckon not," was the crisp answer. "I didn't realize that I was in such bad company."

"But you've only that mucker's word against mine!" cried Bert, flying into another rage.

"I've watched you both, and I'm a pretty good judge of human nature," replied the farmer. "I prefer to believe this young man that you seem to dislike so much."

"You're a nice one---you are!" uttered Bert, glaring in disgust at the ally on whom he had counted.

"Perhaps you can calm down, Dodge, long enough to listen to reason," Dick suggested. "First of all, I am going to admit that we did remove the front tires of your car and that we brought the tires here and hung them on that line."

"Do you hear that?" demanded Dodge eagerly, turning once more to the farmer. "They admit stealing my tires."

"I didn't quite notice that the young man went as far as to admit theft," the farmer replied. "What I heard was that these young men took your tires. As yet I haven't heard their reason for removing the tires of your car."

"The reason for doing so was," Dick went on coolly, "that we had some questions to ask of this fellow Dodge. We knew that if he had to come here to look up his tires, we'd have a chance to ask the questions. Dodge, you thought you were having fun with us when you decorated the entrance to that covered bridge with your notice about a rabid mastiff at large in that part of the country, didn't you? You thought that a mad-dog scare would send us helter-skelter home. If it gives you any satisfaction, I'll admit that the notice did startle us for a brief time. But we soon got at the truth of the matter, and learned that posting the notice was your act."

"Can you prove it?" sneered Dodge.

Ignoring the question, Dick went on:

"Perhaps, had your trick affected only ourselves, then the trick would have been only a piece of meanness without any very serious results. But are you sure, Bert Dodge, that no one but ourselves was alarmed by that notice? Do you know whether any woman traveling over the road may have seen that notice, and then, noticing any strange dog trotting in her direction was frightened, into convulsions, or actually frightened to death? Do you know whether some man, traveling along the road on really important business, read the notice and was afraid to continue on his errand, thereby losing a good deal of money through your foolish trickery? Do you know, for certain, that twenty serious consequences to other people have not followed on the heels of your stupid, senseless joke? Have you any way of being certain that the sheriffs officers are not already searching industriously for the two foolish young fellows who took so many desperate chances in attempting such a 'joke' as that of which you two fellows were guilty?"

"Who's going to prove that Bayliss or I put up that notice?" sneered young Dodge.

"There's at least one witness," Dick answered, "who would testify, at any time, that he passed by you on the road when you were both laughing loudly over a joke you had played. Then there's the notice itself. A handwriting expert could swear that it was done with a pen held by your hand."

"Where's the notice?" asked Bayliss suddenly.

"It's where we can produce it at any time that it's wanted," Prescott made reply. "If anyone has been injured, Dodge, in health or in business, by your stupid, brainless bit of horse play and meanness, then I imagine that you'll find yourself in for a serious time of it. So now you know why we took the tires off your automobile. We knew that our campfire would show you the way to our camp, and that you'd surely be here to hear what we had to say to you. Dodge, we don't care particularly for you, or for Bayliss, either, but if the warning I've given you about pasting up such lying notices to scare people traveling over a public highway is of any use to you, then you're welcome to what you've learned."

The coolness of this proposition was such as to take Bert's breath away for a few seconds. When he recovered, he turned to the red-moustached farmer, sputtering:

"Well, what do you---you think of that cast-iron nerve and cheek?"

"If the facts have been correctly stated," replied the farmer, "I believe these young men have done you a service, and that you'd show more of the spirit of a man if you admitted it."

"Humph!" muttered Dodge.

"Humph!" echoed Bayliss.

Then, enraged at the tantalizing smile on Prescott's face, Bert lost all control of himself.

Striding over, he shook his fist before Dick's face, at the same time shouting:

"All you need is a trimming with fists, and I'm going to give you one---you hound!"

## CHAPTER VI
## PAID IN PULL TO DATE

Then, struck by a sudden consideration of prudence, Bert stepped back two or three feet, looking appealingly at the farmer.

"Will you stay here long enough to see fair play done?" Dodge demanded of the farmer.

"If there is going to be a boxing exhibit, with plenty of science, and all fair play," grinned the farmer, "I don't believe there are enough of you young fellows here to chase me away. Start things moving as soon as you like."

With that the stranger drew out a pipe, which he proceeded to fill and light.

"Get yourself in shape, you mucker!" breathed Bert fiercely, pulling off his coat and tossing his motoring cap after it to the ground. "Come on---get ready!"

"I'm no rowdy," Dick declared coolly, making no move to put himself in readiness.

"No; you're a coward, with a long line of talk, but no spirit in you!" jeered young Dodge.

"If I'm a coward, what possible glory would there be in your fighting me?" Dick smiled.

"Let me have the sneak!" begged Dave, stepping forward, but Dick pushed his churn back. Tom Reade took tight hold of Dave's right arm.

With the prospects of an encounter vanishing, Bert Dodge's valor went up tenfold.

"Get up your guard!" he roared. "I've been taking boxing lessons and I want to teach you one or two things."

"I haven't been taking any boxing lessons lately," Dick remarked with composure.

"Oh, that's why you're afraid to act at all like a man, is it?" scoffed Bert in his harshest voice.

"No; my main reason for not caring to fight you, Dodge, is that I don't like the idea of soiling my hands."

"What's that?" screamed Bert in added fury. "You insult me---you---you mucker?"

"If I'm a mucker, then you don't need to feel insulted at my opinion of you," Dick suggested, with a smile.

But this hesitancy on the part of Prescott was filling Bert Dodge with more valor every instant.

"Prescott, I've owed you something for a mighty long time," quivered Bert. "And now it's coming! Here it is!"

He aimed a savage blow at Dick. Young Prescott, who had really doubted that Dodge had courage enough to invite a fight, was not expecting it. The blow landed on Dick's chin, sending the leader of Dick & Co to the ground.

"Now, get up and answer that---you---you sneak!" dared Bert exultantly.

Dick was on his feet fast enough, side-stepping just in time to dodge a follow-up punch.

"Dodge," Dick remarked, as he threw up his guard, "there, is still time for you to beat it out of here if you don't want to take the consequences of that blow."

"You put me out of here!" Bert retorted defiantly.

Though Dick was quivering with indignation, he still hesitated to spring at Dodge. Dick didn't want to fight, on the sole ground that he felt too much contempt for his opponent.

"Come, on, you mucker!" challenged Bert, dancing about Prescott. Then Dodge delivered two swift, straight-from-the-shoulder blows.

Of a sudden Dick jumped into the fray.

"Good!" quivered Darry, his eyes flashing. To Dave's way of thinking, Dick's swift vigorous defence should have followed that first knock-down.

"Come on, you mucker!" taunted Bert, while the interchange of blows now became fast and furious. "If there's anything you know how to do in this game, let us see what it is! Trot it out!"

"I'll attend to my side of this match," said Dick quietly. "My advice to you is that you keep quiet and save your wind for your own protection."

"Bosh! You can't do anything to anyone in my class!" sneered Bert. Indeed, young Dodge's address to his task opened up particularly well. Dodge was rather heavy for his years, and he had been doing some good training work through the spring and early summer.

Dick, who was lighter and not noticeably quicker, confined himself, at the outset, to his old tactics of allowing his opponent to tire himself.

Bert, however, was soon quick to discover this. He moderated the savagery of his own attack somewhat, sparring cleverly for a chance to feint and then land a face blow.

Dick gave ground readily when it served his purpose, though he did not run.

"Keep back, fellows!" called Tom Reade. "Don't get near enough to interfere with either man."

"Don't interfere with either the man or the thing, you mean," interposed Danny Grin.

"Shut up, Dalzell!" ordered Reade with generous roughness. "Remember that you're not fighting Dodge, and that it's unfair to say anything to anger him. Be fair!"

Though Dick's chums followed the fighters, at a generous distance, they would have noticed, had they been less intent on the work of the combatants, that Bayliss kept well on the outskirts of the crowd. Bayliss didn't want to attract any dangerous notice to himself, nor was he at all sure that the farmer would interfere to see fair play for Dodge's side. In this, however, he really wronged the farmer.

In giving ground Prescott stepped backward, his feet becoming entangled with a vine running along the ground.

Down went Dick, just in time to save himself from a savage blow in the face.

"Stand up to the fight, like a man!" roared Dodge, for he felt that he was winning.

Dick drew himself to his knees. Ere he could gain his feet Bert landed a smashing blow on his left cheek. Down went Dick again.

"Stop that sort of thing, Dodge!" flared Dave Darrin. "Either man who goes down must have safety until he's on his feet again."

"Shut up!" flared Bert, but this time he waited, afraid to try to hit his opponent until Dick was on his feet.

"Can't Dodge run his own fight, hang you?" Bayliss demanded. This was the first word he had had the courage to utter.

Quick as a flash Dave wheeled, running toward Dodge's companion.

"This isn't wholly Dodge's fight, Bayliss," Darry cried, his anger at a white heat. "Prescott has some rights in the game, and you know it, too."

"You're too fresh!" snapped Bayliss.

"You're no good, Bayliss," Darry remarked contemptuously.

"You're a sneak and a liar, and so-----"

"And so I shall claim some of your time just as soon as Dick and Dodge have finished," retorted Darry coldly. "Don't forget that, Bayliss, and don't show your-self up by trying to run away."

With that Darrin stalked back to watch the finish of the present affair.

Dick, on his feet again, renewed the battle in earnest. He found Dodge a really worthy opponent. Both boys soon had bruised faces to show.

Smash! That blow, delivered by Bert, almost ended the fight. Dick staggered backward, the blood beginning to flow from his nose.

Dodge followed it up, driving in another hard blow. The pain stung Dick, not to madness, but into a more resolute defense, with more of offense in it.

Then Dick so manoeuvred that he had Dodge between himself and the shore of the lake. This advantage gave young Prescott slightly higher ground on the gentle slope toward the lake. Bert tried to manoeuvre for a more level footing, but Prescott drove him slowly backward.

Suddenly one of Dick's blows landed, with staggering force, on the tip of Dodge's chin. Bert went to earth, rolling over as he struck, and lying face down-ward. He was not knocked out, but he had had enough.

For a moment or two Dick glanced down at his adversary in cold contempt. Then suddenly, without a word, he bent over, seizing Dodge by the shirt collar and belt, and threw him sprawling out into the lake.

Young Dodge landed some distance from the bank. There was a loud splash and a yell from the vanquished one, then a gurgling noise as Bert's mouth went under water. He disappeared under the black surface of the lake.

Dick waited calmly, ready to go to Dodge's assistance if needed. Bert, however, rose quickly, the water not much above his knees.

"You loafer!" hissed Dodge, dashing the water from his face.

"Haven't you had enough?" asked Prescott mildly. "Didn't the water cool you off?"

Dodge didn't reply, but he walked a few steps away before attempting to step on dry land, thus avoiding his late opponent.

"That little business is all over," declared Tom Reade coolly. "Bend down by the water, Dick, and I'll wash your nose with my handkerchief. Greg, bring one of the lanterns here."

"Now, I guess it's time for our practice, Bayliss," Dave announced, stepping over to Bert's companion.

"I've got to look after Dodge," mumbled Bayliss.

"No, you don't!" Dave warned him. "After the kind of language you have used to me you can't slip out of trouble quite so easily as all that. Get ready."

"Quit---can't you?" protested Bayliss.

"No; not unless you'll admit that you lied when you applied disagreeable names to me," said Dave Darrin firmly. "Bayliss, are you ready to admit that you are a liar?"

"You bet I'm not!" cried the other hoarsely. "Then back up your words! Ready! Here's something coming!"

That "something" arrived. Bayliss fairly gasped as Darrin started in on him.

But Dave drew back, holding up his fists.

"You didn't get started fairly, Bayliss," Darry declared. "I want you to have as fair a show as possible. Draw in a deep breath. Fill your lungs with air. Plant your feet firmly. Put up your hands."

Patiently Darry waited for perhaps three quarters of a minute.

"Now!" he said at last.

Then the fight went on, but it was one sided. Had Bayliss done himself justice, it might have resulted in a draw, at least, for Bayliss was strong and quick. But he lacked courage.

Presently Bayliss, considerably battered, though not as severely punished as Dodge had been, went down to his knees, nor would he rise.

"Going to get up and go on?" demanded Darry, pausing before him. "Or do you quit?"

Bayliss, breathing hard, did not answer.

"What you need here," declared the farmer, stepping forward and puffing slowly at his pipe, "is a referee. I'll take the job. Bayliss, if you believe that you can do anything more, then the place for you is on your feet. I'll give you until I count five."

Deliberately the farmer counted, but Bayliss remained on his knees.

"Bayliss loses," announced the farmer. "Not that I believe he ever had much in the fighting line to lose, but he loses."

"I'll wait five minutes for him," offered Darry. "By that time he'll be in shape to go on again."

"He's in good enough shape now," declared the self-appointed referee. "The point is that Mr. Bayliss hasn't any liking for boxing. He's the kind of young man that finds croquet strenuous enough!"

The four recent combatants now had some repairing to do. Dick and Dave were attended by their own friends. The farmer offered to help Bert Dodge ease his bruises. Greg made a tender of his services to Bayliss, but was gruffly repulsed.

"Everything is over," called the farmer at last. "I must wake up my horses and get on to Gridley. Young gentlemen, I'm much obliged for the rest that my horses have had, and also for my entertainment. Dodge, I don't believe you're really worth an ounce of soda crackers, but I realize that you don't feel as bright as usual, so I'm going to help you get the tires on your car."

Reaching up, the farmer untied one end of the line on which the tires hung. Letting the tubes fall at his feet. The man then drew a card out of his pocket and handed it to Reade.

"That will tell you who I am, if you ever want to find me," suggested the farmer.

"George Simpson," said Tom, reading the card. "Mr. Simpson, we're certainly glad of having had the pleasure of meeting you."

Reade thereupon gravely introduced the other members of Dick & Co.

"Glad to have met you, boys," said Simpson, picking up the tires. "Now, come along, Dodge and Bayliss, if you want my help, for I really must be moving."

"This hasn't been such a dull evening, after all," jovially commented Tom Reade, after the late visitors had vanished into the darkness surrounding the camp.

"I'm sorry for the fighting, though," mused Dick aloud. "I don't enjoy anything that makes bad blood, or more bad blood, between human beings."

"You couldn't do anything else but fight," retorted Greg sharply.

"That's the only reason why I fought," Prescott rejoined.

Half or three quarters of an hour later two resonant honks sounded from the red Smattach automobile up at the roadside. Dick & Co. rightly judged that Simpson had taken this means of signaling them that the Smattach car was ready to go on its way again.

"What's the matter with Mr. Simpson?" Tom demanded at the top of his voice.

From the throats of all of Dick & Co. came the ready response!

"He's all right!"

Honk! honk! honk! Mr. Simpson had heard this tribute to himself. Then the chugging of a starting car was heard. The noise soon sounded fainter, then died away.

"That's the last of the firm of Dodge and Bayliss for this season!" chuckled Dave Darrin.

In this conclusion, however, it was wholly probable that Darry was wrong. He would have been sure of it, himself, had he been privileged to hear the talk of Bert Dodge and his companion as the enraged and humiliated pair drove swiftly over the rough road on their way back to Gridley.

"I can't think of anything bad enough to call Dick Prescott," growled Bert, who sat at the steering wheel.

"Don't try to," grumbled Bayliss. "It would poison your mind."

"The mucker!"

"The sneak!"

"The coward! He fights only when he has his gang with him."

"I don't see what the high school fellows can find to admire in that crowd," quivered Bayliss, tenderly fingering his damaged eye.

"Never mind what anyone thinks of them!" raged Bert Dodge. "We've nothing but our own side of the affair to settle!"

"What do you mean?" asked Bayliss curiously.

"Bayliss, what do you think I am?"

"Oh, I guess you're a pretty good sort of fellow, Bert."

"Do you think I'd let business like to-night's go by without resenting it?"

"Are you going to try to take Prescott on again?" Bayliss asked wonderingly.

"I'm not a fool!" retorted Dodge indignantly. "Prescott might thrash me again. Bayliss, I'm going to hit him with the kind of club that he can't beat!"

"Is the club big enough to take care of Darrin, too?"

"I'm after the whole Prescott gang, for good measure!" Bert raged.

"What are you going to do?"

"I'll let you in on it, Bayliss, when I have all the details planned---if you've nerve enough to do a man's part---of which I'm not too sure," Dodge finished under his breath.

"You may count on me for anything---anything that is prudent!" Bayliss declared.

## CHAPTER VII
## THE BOX THAT SET THEM GUESSING

L ook at that!" cried Tom Reade, leaping up from the breakfast table so precipitately that he overturned his cup of coffee.

"What?" demanded Greg.

"Didn't you see that---out on the lake?" Tom demanded.

"I didn't see anything," Greg admitted.

"There it goes again!" cried Tom.

"Oh, I saw something rise from the water and fall back again," continued Greg.

"Do you know what it was?" Reade insisted.

"No."

"That was a black bass!" declared Reade, as though it were one of the seven wonders of the world.

"Keep cool, Reade," chaffed Danny Grin. "We all knew, that there are fish in the lake."

"But black bass-----" choked Tom.

"Are they any better eating than any other fish?" asked Hazelton.

"Not so much better," Reade confessed. "But black bass are gamey, and hard fish to land when you hook 'em!"

"They're no better food, but it's harder work to get them," laughed Greg. "Sit down, Tom, and keep cool"

"No real fisherman would ever talk that way," Tom insisted indignantly. "The greatest charm about fishing comes in hooking and landing the really good fighting fish!"

"How much does a black bass weigh?" asked Greg.

"That one probably weighed four pounds. Look! look! There he goes again.

Did you fellows see him?"

"There isn't any four pound fish in water that can give me a fight," Danny Grin asserted solemnly. "I'd be ashamed to talk about having a fight with a four pound fish. It looks small and mean to me."

"Well, go after some bass, if they're so easy to catch," urged Greg. "I'll look on and see if you've over estimated your ability as a fisherman."

"You're a fine fisherman, aren't you?" demanded Tom scornfully.

"No fisherman at all," Holmes promptly confessed.

"If you knew the A-B-C of fishing," Reade continued, "you'd know that one must have a boat in order to go after bass."

"Don't they ever come near enough to shore to be caught without the aid of a boat?" Danny Grin demanded.

Tom snorted.

"Tell me," insisted Dalzell.

"You're stringing me," protested Tom.

"No; I'm after information," Dan asserted.

"If you really don't know," Tom resumed, "I'll tell you that black bass are generally caught only by trolling for them. That is, if I fish for bass I've got to keep playing my line over the stern while someone else rows the boat."

"You've a positive genius for picking out the easy half of the job," Danny Grin murmured admiringly.

"The trolling part of the job merely looks easy," Tom went on, good-humoredly. "The fellow who is doing the fisherman act must have all the brains, while the fellow at the oars may be a real dolt, for all he has to know. I'll take you out with me after black bass, Danny, if we can get hold of a boat one of these days."

"Who'll do the rowing?" asked Dalzell suspiciously.

"Naturally you will," was Reade's answer.

"Can't we find a boat somewhere about here?" asked Hazelton eagerly.

"I haven't seen one on any part of the lake that is visible from here," Prescott put in. "I don't know why, but this so called second lake doesn't seem to be a popular spot. There isn't a house to be seen anywhere along the shore on either side, and I doubt if there's a boat on this sheet of water."

"I don't believe there is a boat, either---and just look at that!" cried Reade, as three distinct splashes about an eighth of a mile out showed how frequently the bass were leaping.

"It's tough---not to have a chance at good sport!" declared Dave Darrin impatiently. "We fellows ought to search this old shore, anyway, to see if we can't find some sort of craft."

"Come along, then!" urged Tom, leaping to his feet. "I can't stand this state of affairs much longer. Look at that, out there. Four bass jumping within fifteen seconds. This is cruelty to fishermen!"

"Tom, you take Dan and Harry, and go up along the shore," proposed Dick. "I'll take the others with me, and we'll go down along the shore. Each party will walk and search for half an hour, and then return, unless we find a boat sooner."

"Aren't you going to leave someone to watch the camp?" asked Danny Grin.

"It is hardly necessary," decided Prescott.

"But Bert Dodge-----" suggested Greg.

"For Dodge to be out here so early he'd have to be up by five in the morning, and make an early start," Dick rejoined. "I don't believe he's industrious enough for that."

"The camp will be all right," Dave agreed.

"Of course," Tom assented. "Anyway, there's nothing here worth stealing that would be small enough to carry away."

"Except the food," hinted Danny Grin.

"This is too far off the main roads for tramps to come this way," Dick replied.

So Dalzell, with a sigh, rose to accompany Reade and Hazelton.

Dick and his two companions thoroughly explored the shore as far as they went on the lower part of the lake. From time to time Prescott consulted his watch. In all the time that they were out they passed only one building, a tumble-down, weather-beaten shack that looked as though it had not been inhabited in twenty years. Not even a vestige of a craft was found.

"It's time to go back," said Dick at last. "Too bad we couldn't find anything."

"There must have been boats on this lake at one time," hinted Dave, "or else there wouldn't be that broken-down old pier near the camp."

"I guess there was a time when this lake was a fishing ground to supply the Gridley and other near-by markets," Dick went on. "But, fellows, there's a curious thing about these fish markets that I don't know whether you've noticed. There are several fish stores in Gridley, and yet in all of them you couldn't buy a pound of fish except the kinds that are caught in salt water. I wonder if there are any fish markets in this part of the country that make a specialty of fresh-water fish?"

More slowly, Dick, Dave and Greg retraced their steps.

"Hoo-hoo! Hoo-hoo!" signaled Dick as they neared their camp.

From away up the shore the answering "hoo hoo!" came faintly.

"Tom didn't give up the search as easily as we did," commented Dave. "Poor old chap, he will be seriously disappointed if he hasn't found something that will float. He's the one sincere fisherman of the crowd, and the bass certainly have hypnotized him."

"Race you back to camp," offered Dick.

"Come back," laughed Dave, "and make a fair start."

But Dick kept on, laughing back at his distanced comrades. Prescott ran like a deer, as was to be expected from one who had played left end on the invincible Gridley High School eleven.

Just as he bounded on to the camp ground Dick's glance fell on a packing box some four feet long.

"This doesn't belong here," he muttered, bounding forward, then dropping on one knee beside the box.

In amazed wonder he read the following inscription, from a card tacked to the box:

"Will Dick Prescott accept the enclosed and keep it as trustee for Dick & Co.? From a most appreciative friend---two of them, in fact!"

"Now, what on earth can this be?" Dick demanded, as Dave reached his side.

Darry read the message on the card with growing wonder.

"Greg," directed Dick, "trot into the camp and get a hammer and the cold chisel. Hustle!"

Full of curiosity, Greg Holmes carried out the order at a run.

"Here you are!" panted Holmes.

Dick took the cold chisel, placed the edge against one side of the lid, and was about to strike the first blow when Darry snatched the hammer from his hand.

"What ails you?" Prescott demanded.

"Suspicion," Dave replied dryly. "In fact, I've a bad case of suspiciousness."

"What are you talking about?" Dick insisted.

"I don't know," Dave admitted. "But I've something of a shivery hunch that perhaps we'd better not open that box."

"What, then? Toss it into the lake?"

"Even that might not be as foolish as it sounds to you," Darry went on. "How do we know what that box contains!"

"We never will know until we open it," declared Greg impatiently.

"And then we might be mighty sorry that we opened it," Dave continued.

"You think that there is something suspicious about the box?" queried Prescott.

"Oh, the box looks all right," Dave laughed. "But the contents might prove more than a disappointment. A real danger, for instance."

"Do you really think so?" Dick mused wonderingly.

"Well, let's not be too rash," Darrin urged. "When I try to think of the friends who might take the trouble to come away out here to leave something for us, about the dearest friends I can think of are---Dodge and Bayliss."

"And what would they leave in the box for us?" pondered Prescott.

"Anything from a nest of rattlesnakes to an infernal machine," Greg Holmes suggested.

"That doesn't sound quite reasonable," Dick replied slowly. "Neither Dodge nor Bayliss amount to much, and both fellows are pretty mean; but do you imagine they would dare do anything that might come very close to murder? I don't."

"Oh, well, open the box, then," Dave agreed. "Whatever may be in it of a dangerous nature, I'll stand by and take my share of it."

"A few minutes won't make any difference," said Dick, rising and dropping hammer and chisel. "We'll wait until the rest of the fellows come in, and then we'll hold a pow-wow and vote on what's to be done."

"Tom! Oh, Tom! Fellows! Hoo-hoo!" roared Greg, making a megaphone of his hands.

"Wha-at's wa-anted?" came Reade's hail, still from a distance.

"Hurry up!" yelled Greg. "Hustle. Big doings here!"

"Have you found a boat?" came Tom's query.

"No! But---hustle! Run!"

Greg was alive with curiosity. He could not wait. If the box were to be opened only after a pow-wow, then the sooner the council were held the sooner the mystery of the box's contents would be solved.

Tom, Dan and Harry came in at a trot.

"What's all the row about?" Reade demanded.

"That," stated Greg, pointing to the packing case.

"What's in it?" asked Reade.

"We don't know," said Dick.

"I fail to see what's to hinder you from knowing," retorted Reade. "I see that you have the tools for opening the case at hand. What were you waiting for---my strong arm on the hammer? If so-----"

While speaking Tom had been glancing at the inscription on the card.

"I don't know just whether we ought to open it," Dave declared. "That box may come from Dodge and Bayliss, and we may be sorry that we meddled with it."

"There may be something in that," agreed Reade, laying down hammer and chisel and rising. "But I wish we knew."

"We all wish that," said Greg.

"Well, what are we going to do?" inquired Hazelton. "Are we going to remain afraid of the box and shy away from it?"

"I'm not afraid," replied Darrin, his color rising. "I'm willing to open it if you fellows say so."

"Then what has kept you back so far?" Tom wanted to know.

"If it's a job put up by Dodge and Bayliss, then I don't just like to be caught napping by them," Dave replied. "However, you fellows all get back a few rods---and here goes for little David to solve the box mystery."

"Not!" advised Reade with emphasis. "I suppose we'll have to do something with this box, sometime, but I, for one, am in favor of considering the matter for a little while before we go any further. Dave, you are a foxy one, but I'm glad you are. It may save us all trouble."

So the box lay there through the forenoon, and Dick & Co. did little else but wonder and guess as to its contents.

Any member of Dick & Co. would have taken the risk of opening it, had he been chosen by his comrades to do so; but not one of them wanted one of the other fellows to take the risk.

In the meantime Greg Holmes could scarcely curb his rising curiosity.

## CHAPTER VIII
## THE MAN WITH THE HAUNTING FACE

The noon meal had been eaten, and the camp put to rights. The water before them and the woods behind them called to nature-loving Dick & Co., yet the invitations were ignored.

What could be in the innocent-looking box? That was the question that held six minds in the thraldom of curiosity.

"I can't stand this suspense any longer!" muttered Reade towards three o'clock in the afternoon.

"Open the box yourself," prompted Danny Grin.

"I will," offered Reade, advancing toward the box. "I don't care if it's a ton of dynamite, all fixed up with clock work and automatic fuses. I want to find it out."

But Greg Holmes sprang forward.

"Wait just a little longer, Tom," he urged. "Dick will be back in a few minutes and then we'll get him to agree to it."

"Dick Prescott doesn't open the box," Tom retorted.

"It's addressed to him, anyway," said Greg firmly.

"I guess that's right," interposed Dave, nodding. "And Dick will be here soon."

Dick reappeared within five minutes. He had taken two buckets and had gone to a spring at some distance from camp for water.

"Dick," said Greg, "there's Tom on the ground on the other side of that tree. He's growling like a Teddy bear because no one has opened the box."

"I think we'd better open it," nodded Prescott, after glancing at the faces of the others, for he saw that their curiosity was at fever heat.

"Hooray!" yelled Greg. "Come on, fellows!"

There was a rush for the hammer and cold chisel, but young Holmes won.

"You pry the lid up on one side, and then give me a chance at the other side," proposed Tom Reade.

But Greg, smiling quietly, soon had the entire lid off the box.

Nothing but a lot of multi-colored, curly packing paper met their gaze.

"The world destroyer must be underneath this ton of rubbish," grunted Darry, kneeling and prying the strings of paper out.

At last he delved down to a parcel wrapped in stout manila paper and securely tied with cord.

"Cut the strings," advised Reade, passing Dave a pocket knife with one blade open.

Darrin, however, had lifted the parcel out to lay it on the ground. It was fairly heavy, but Dave handled it with ease. Now he cut the strings. As the papers were pushed aside he and the others saw nothing at first but a lot of khaki-colored canvas.

"Fellows," declared Dick, "I don't believe this is a practical joke, at all. It looks to me as though someone had sent us something very much like a cook tent."

All thought of danger having now passed, Prescott and his comrades unfolded the canvas. At the bottom of the package they found something that caused them to send up a wild hurrah.

Two daintily modeled white maple paddles lay there. There were two other objects made of wood that looked like seats.

"Fellows," gasped Dick, "don't you understand what this is?"

"I do," nodded Tom huskily. "I do, if not another soul in the world does. Fellows, it's a collapsible canoe, all ready to set up and run into the water. It's our boat, that we've been wanting so badly. It's a beauty! Oh, shake it out! Lay it and let's put the braces in! I shan't be able to breathe again until I see this thing of beauty floating on the water!"

Yet Tom was no more excited than were the other members of Dick & Co. All took a hand, and all tried to work so nimbly that they got considerably in the way of one another. Yet at last the canoe was ready to be picked up and carried to the lake's edge.

"Here's even a painter to tie it to a tree with," shouted Dave. "Say! Whoever bought this canoe knew all about one!"

"Don't anyone try to get into the craft yet," ordered Dick, as the canoe was slid out upon the water, Prescott holding the painter, which he tied around a sapling growing near the water's edge. "We want to make sure that this canoe is water-proof. If it stands twenty minutes without taking in water we'll know it's all right."

Since they couldn't board the canoe, these delighted boys joined hands, dancing about in a ring. Then, suddenly, they started off in burlesqued figures of an Indian war-dance, whooping like mad.

While the excitement was at its height, Reade suddenly seized Hazelton by his collar, rushing him to the lake. Into it went both boys, Tom ducking Harry's head under the water.

"Wha-a-at's that for?" sputtered Hazelton as soon as he could talk.

"Because you needed it," replied Tom soberly. "Will you kindly do as much for me? We were all such chumps that we cheated ourselves out of the best black bass fishing to-day that ever mortal saw. So we all ought to be ducked."

Harry stared at his friend in some astonishment.

"On second thought, though," concluded Reade, "you needn't duck me. You may postpone it. I'm going bass fishing the very instant that the canoe is judged to be safe."

"And I'll be the bass-hunting pin-head who merely does the paddling," proposed Danny Grin meekly.

"I guess you're the biggest pin-head in camp, all right---after myself," nodded Reade. "So we ought to hit it off as bass fishermen, Danny boy."

"Fellows," hinted Dick judicially, "I think we had better turn the canoe over to Tom for the first trip. His craze to go bass fishing is so acute that it fairly pains him. Tom can have the first trip, can't he?"

There was a general assent. Tom darted away to overhaul such tackle as he had for bass fishing. He came back with a small but tough jointed rod, some very long lines, and some flashily, bright spoons.

"Danny, get a shovel and dig for some grubs," Tom ordered, as he sorted tackle. "When you can't fool black bass with one thing you must try another. If you fellows see any tiny chubs swimming about in the little coves here, try to get a lot of them. We can keep them in a bucket of water. Perch? Bah! The real fishing is about to begin now!"

"Do you really expect to get any bass today, Tom?" Dick inquired.

"Hard to say," replied Reade, shaking his head as he glanced up from the tackle he was overhauling to look out upon the lake. "I haven't seen a single bass jump in five hours now. But I may get two or three. I certainly will, if the bass are sportsmanlike enough to give me any show at 'em."

By the time that Tom had his tackle in shape Dick and Dave pronounced the canoe wholly water tight. Dan Dalzell, equipped with one of the paddles, took a kneeling position just back of the bow seat. Tom got in next, squatting with his face to the stern of the canoe. None of the others were to go. At a pinch this ten-foot canoe might hold three, but fishermen as a rule do not care to have extra passengers in their boats.

"Give 'em a cheer, boys!" cried Darry, as Danny Grin, with a few deft strokes of the paddle, propelled the craft away from the shore.

"And let that cheer be the last," called back Tom, in a low voice that nevertheless traveled backward over the water. "Don't frighten my bass from coming up to take a look at me."

"Tom surely is the sincere old bass fisher, isn't he?" demanded Harry Hazelton.

"I don't know," Dick made answer. "We can tell better when we've seen him hook and land a few fish."

"Paddle slowly right across the lake, Danny," begged Tom, watching his trolling line.

From the camp the boys watched until they grew tired of the monotony. Reade did not seem destined to secure a single "strike" from bass that afternoon.

"At half-past four o'clock," proposed Darrin, "I'll go down to the old pier and see what I can do toward catching a string of perch for to-night."

"I'll go with you," nodded Hazelton.

"All right," agreed Dick. "Greg and I will get in the water and wood, and see to whatever else we're to have for supper. I don't believe Tom will bring us anything."

Nor did Reade himself believe it. For two solid hours Dan Dalzell paddled lazily wherever his skipper told him to. The nearest that Tom seemed destined to get a "strike" was when his hook caught in the weeds.

At last they were some distance out on the lake, perhaps a hundred and fifty yards from shore. Reade, wholly discouraged, was about to give the order to make for camp.

Turning about in the canoe, Reade discovered that Dalzell was in a brown study, slowly lifting his paddle and lifting it out again, but without watching his course.

"Look out, Danny boy," cautioned Tom, "or you'll scratch the sides of the canoe on those bushes right ahead."

Dan glanced up with a start, backing water. They had now passed in under the shadow of trees, for the sun was low, and it was somewhat dark and gloomy in there.

"It's queer for bushes to be growing so far out from shore," muttered Tom, "and it shows how shallow the water must be about here. You had better back water out of here, Danny."

Dalzell was about to do so when his glance fell on something that halted his arm.

In the same moment Tom Reade saw the object that had arrested Dan's attention.

From between the bushes peered a pair of deep-set, frightened eyes that looked out from the haggard, despairing face of a man whose head alone was visible.

Just for the moment neither Tom nor Dalzell could really guess whether the face belonged to the living or the dead. The sight caused cold shivers to run up and down their spines, for that face was ghastly and haunting in the extreme.

But quickly Tom Reade found his voice sufficiently to ask huskily:

"What's your trouble, my friend?"

## CHAPTER IX
## THE START OF A BAD NIGHT

Without noise, leaving barely a ripple behind, that head sank from view. It had vanished in an instant before the eyes of the two thoroughly startled high school boys.

"He's drowning now!" gasped Dan, as the head failed to bob up again into view. "Oh, Tom, we must save him!"

"Wait!" said Reade, in a quivering voice. His eyes expressed uncertainty as to how he should act.

"But he's drowning. You see, he hasn't come up again!" Dalzell insisted.

"Drowning---in water shallow enough for small bushes to grow from the bottom?" demanded Reade. "Of course not! But what does it mean---and why didn't the fellow speak?"

"Perhaps---i---i---it was a---dead man," suggested Dalzell.

"That's what I'm trying to figure out," replied Reade. "I---I almost thought I saw the man's eyelids move."

"I thought so, too," agreed Dan, "but now I'm inclined to believe that we didn't. Wait! I'm going to get close to the bushes."

Dan drove the paddle into the water a few times, bringing the canoe up alongside the bushes, when it was seen that these were standing up from a square framework of wood.

"Now, what do you think of that?" asked Reade in perplexity. "These are freshly cut bushes, that have been fastened to this frame to-day. The frame will float wherever wind or current may take it. I thought this was shallow water. I'll soon know."

Tom had, among his tackle, a line with a sinker attached. He tossed the sinker over the side of the canoe, paying out the line until the sinker touched bottom. Then he pulled the line in again, carefully measuring by his arm as much of the line as was wet.

"Danny," he announced solemnly, "at this point the water is from twenty-seven to thirty feet deep."

"Then that man did drown!" breathed Dalzell, his face as white as chalk.

"Of course he did," Tom agreed, "provided he was alive when we saw him."

"But he had to be alive," protested Dan, "or else he couldn't have nailed the framework together and decorated it with branches from bushes."

"That is, if the man we saw made the frame," propounded Reade in a very solemn voice.

It was a shock to both of them. The whole incident had been uncanny and unreal, but the horror of that haggard, haunting face was still strong upon both of the beholders.

"Tom, we simply must get off our clothes and dive to see what we can do to find that poor fellow," urged Dalzell.

"All right," assented Reade. "I'll do all the diving myself, Danny, if you'll take command and give your orders. Where shall I dive? The bushes have already shifted position. We're floating away from the spot, too. Just where do you want me to make the first dive?"

"I don't know," Dan Dalzell confessed. "The whole affair has given me the creeps, I think."

"I know it has done that to me," smiled Tom unsteadily. "Whew! I'll dream of that face to-night---all night long! Dan, there seems to be just about one chance in a thousand that that man will reach shore. Let's keep the craft headed to the shore, and watch for some minutes to come. At the same time, if we see a sign of the poor fellow, we'll swim to him, or paddle to him as fast as we know how."

Both boys knew, inwardly, that they would be heartily glad to get away from what seemed plainly to them to be a haunted spot. Yet neither cared to admit his dread to the other. So, talking rather busily, they remained on the spot for fully another ten minutes.

"We won't see anything come out of the water now," Tom asserted at last. "Even if we do, it will be a drowned man."

"I guess we may as well get back to camp," Danny agreed. "Yet it is going to be an awfully creepy night for all of us, with this weird mystery of the lake on our minds."

"Don't paddle yet," begged Tom. "I'll give a hail, and see if that brings any answer."

Raising his voice, Reade shouted lustily:

"Hello, there, friend? Are you safe? Want any help?"

"Anything we can do for you, friend?" bawled Dan Dalzell, in his most resonant tone.

Only the mocking echoes of their own questions came back to them.

"Beat the water with the paddle. Danny," advised Reade after they had waited for some moments. "We've more than a mile to go. Whip up the water. If you get tired, pass the paddle back to me."

"I'm not sorry to get away from that place," breathed Dalzell, after at least a hundred lusty strokes.

"Nor I," confessed Reade. "I'm beginning to get a headache already from trying to figure out what it all meant. Danny, describe that haunting face just as you saw it."

"Ugh! I hate to think about it again," protested Dalzell.

"You'll think about it more than once," retorted Tom. "You won't be able to help that, I promise you. So go ahead and describe the face as you saw it."

Dan did so, Tom listening attentively.

"Then that wasn't a case of imagination," Tom declared gravely. "If we had imagined it, each would have seen a different face. But the face that you describe, Danny, is the one that I also saw. Pass back the paddle, please. I want a little exercise."

Tom still had the paddle when he shot the canoe in close to the camp.

"Any luck?" called Dave, who had already returned with a string of perch.

"Catch any bass?" was Dick's question.

"Did you even see anything?" laughed Greg Holmes.

"Did we see anything?" groaned Tom, as he sent the canoe's prow to land.

"Danny looks as though he had been seeing all sorts of things," chuckled Hazelton, as Dalzell stepped ashore.

"Don't ask me," gasped Danny Grin, with a shudder.

At this the faces of those who had remained behind sobered instantly.

"You won't eat any supper, if we tell you," Tom declared, as he came ashore while Dave held the painter of the canoe.

"I'll accept that challenge," laughed Prescott, as Dave and Tom drew the collapsible canoe up on shore. "Fire away as soon as you're ready, Mr. Reade."

Perch and potatoes were frying, coffee bubbling and Dick had been mixing some kind of boiled pudding that he had learned to make so that it would not cause acute indigestion.

"Better wait until after supper," Reade advised.

"No; we want the story now," Prescott declared firmly.

So Reade told of the strange apparition they had seen, with many additions to the tale from Danny.

"I decline to shudder," asserted Dave.

"That's just because you've only heard about the face, instead of seeing it," Tom muttered.

"Dick, what do you make of the whole affair?" asked Greg.

"I only wish I could guess the answer," Prescott made answer solemnly, "but I can't."

"What are we going to do about it?" asked Tom Reade.

"Let it alone," proposed Harry Hazelton.

"No, we won't," said Dick promptly. "Not unless we have to, just because of inability to find out anything. Fellows, it's too late to try to do anything in the darkness to-night. If the man were drowned, we couldn't help him, anyway. But we'll go over there to-morrow and try to find out whether there is any other answer to the riddle."

"You won't need any supper to-night, anyway," declared Reade, in a tone of grim triumph.

"That is where you lose," Prescott answered quietly. "You'll be hungry, too, Tom, when the food goes on the table."

However, neither Reade nor Danny Grin ate very heartily that evening. Every few moments the haunting face rose before their memories. It proved a dull evening, too, in camp. The sky became overcast. It looked so much like rain that Dick

& Co. voted in favor of retiring early.

First of all, however, the canoe was hauled into the tent for safety. Then, with only one lantern burning dimly, six sturdy but wondering high school boys rolled themselves in their blankets.

Just as five of them were dozing off uneasily Dave Darrin's voice sounded quietly:

"That thing couldn't have been a joke rigged up on us, could it?"

"A joke?" rumbled Reade. "No, sir! That face was real enough to suit the most particular individual. No, sir; that face wasn't a joke, nor did the face look as though the man to whom it belonged had ever heard a joke in all his life."

"Suppose you fellows shut up until the sun is shining again," proposed Danny Grin, who had been fidgeting restlessly in his blanket.

"That's right," agreed Dick blandly. "All ghost stories ought to be told in the broad daylight."

"Just the same-----" Tom began.

"Shut up---*please*!" came a chorus of protest.

All was quiet after that. Hours must have passed. All the boys were sleeping at least fairly well when air and earth shook with a mighty explosion.

Instantly six bewildered high school boys leaped to their feet in alarm.

# CHAPTER X
# POWDER MILLS, OR JUST WHAT?

I f that's a thunderstorm," muttered Greg Holmes, barely half awake, "then it's going to be a dandy!"

But Dick seized him by one arm and shook him.

"Come to your senses, Greg! That wasn't thunder."

"No; but what was it?" wondered Dave.

"I'm going to dress and find out," rejoined Dick sturdily. He sat on the edge of his canvas cot and began to pull on his clothing.

BANG! All were awake enough now to appreciate fully the force of this second jarring explosion.

"I wonder if there are any powder works off in this wilderness?" asked Danny Grin.

But Dick, who had now dressed as fully as he intended to do, save for the lacing of his shoes, now came back from the doorway of the tent with the lantern, the wick of which he was turning up.

"No powder mills in this part of the world," he declared. "But, gracious! The explosion seemed big enough."

Tom Reade stepped over to Prescott, whispering in the latter's ear:

"What if this is another chapter in the lake mystery that we struck this afternoon?"

"That's possible," nodded Dick.

"What are you two fellows whispering about?" called Hazelton.

"We're using whispers in case there's anyone else near enough to hear speaking voices," Prescott explained in a low tone.

That was enough to fan the curiosity of the others, who, partially dressed, crowded about Prescott and Reade.

Leaving the lantern in the tent, Dick & Co. gathered in the darkness in the open air.

"What do you make of it, Dick?" Dave asked.

"Just as much as you fellows do---no more," came the reply.

"If it isn't anything that carries danger to us," proposed Darrin, "we may as well go back and to bed."

"All who are sleepy enough may go back and turn in," Prescott suggested. "I'll stay up and watch for a while."

"So will I," promised Reade.

But it turned out that none of the party wanted to sleep. Even Darrin said he was interested enough in this newest mystery to stay up and try to fathom it.

"Whatever it is," smiled Dick, "it hasn't done us any harm."

"Oh, yes; there has been one casualty, at least," protested Holmes. "The explosion has caused a compound fracture in my bump of curiosity."

"There don't seem to be any more explosions," suggested Dick Prescott, after a few moments had passed, and some of the boys were yawning. "Anyone want to turn in?"

No one wished to do so, however.

"If we can't find out anything to-night," murmured Dick, in a low voice, "we'll at least make a strong effort in that direction after breakfast to-morrow morning."

"We have the lake mystery on for after breakfast," urged Hazelton.

"There's probably a connection between the lake mystery and the big explosions," whispered Tom Reade wisely. "Fellows, I've a notion that Danny Grin and I unintentionally bumped into someone else's business of some queer kind. Now the people who are peevish with us are trying to chase us out of these woods. At least, that's my idea."

"It will take something more than noise to chase us," smiled Dick coolly. "Our ear drums are as sound as the next fellow's. Just the same, I wish we might find out something about this mystery. If there's another explosion like that last one, then some of us ought to travel straight in the direction of the noise."

"And run straight into the hard, swift punch that is behind that noise!" muttered Danny Grin, with one of those facial contortions that had earned him his nickname.

"Whoever starts to playing with a boy's curiosity must be ready to abide by the consequences," chuckled Prescott. "Now, if anyone has started something against us, then we'll run the rascal to the earth."

"You don't suppose it's Dodge's work?" whispered Greg.

Before Dick could answer Darrin broke in with an emphatic:

"Not much! The lake mystery affair is one of too large calibre for Bert Dodge's poor, anaemic brain. There's something bigger and smarter than a mere Dodge behind the doings of this night."

"It's one o'clock, fellows," said Dick, after walking over to the lantern for a glimpse at his watch. "Tom, Greg and I will stay up until three o'clock and be ready to jump out together at the first sign of anything happening. The rest of you turn in and get some sleep. We'll call you at three o'clock and then take our turn at the pillow."

"You'll call us, of course, if anything happens?" asked Dave.

"If another powder mill blows up," chuckled Tom, "you won't need to be called. You'll be out here on the jump."

Dave, Dan and Harry thereupon turned in. Knowing that others were on watch the trio in the tent were all sound asleep within five minutes.

Only the sighing of the wind through the trees, the occasional splash of a leaping fish in the lake, and the subdued, musical hum of tiny night insects came to the ears of Dick and his fellow watchers.

Greg was soon yawning. Tom, for want of something better to do, began describing all over again the strange apparition he and Dalzell had seen that afternoon. Greg, finding the "creeps" in Tom's narration to be stronger than the interest, shivered and withdrew to a spot beyond the reach of Tom's whispers.

Not long after Greg, his back propped against a tree trunk, was sound asleep.

Tom liked to talk. Prescott was a good listener, putting in a question now and then.

So at least another hour passed. Then-----

Boo-oom!

That crash was so close at hand that it seemed as though the earth must open.

Tom's first startled glance was at the sky. Then, with a whisking sound, several fragments of something passed over their heads.

"We're being bombarded?" gasped Tom inquiringly.

"This is getting too noisy to be interesting," protested Greg, waking and leaping over to the place where his chums stood.

"I thought you fellows were going to put a stop to that racket!" complained Darry from the tent.

Dick Prescott's whole thought and effort had been centered on the task of placing the location of that latest explosion.

"You fellows look after the camp," Dick called in a low voice to those in the tent. "Come on, Tom and Greg!"

His two chums hurried to overtake him as the young leader rushed off in the darkness. Prescott was traveling up the slope in a direction that ran in an oblique line from the lake front.

"Are you sure it was just exactly in this direction?" whispered Reade, as he reached Dick's side.

"In this direction as nearly as I could judge," Dick affirmed.

For some moments they traveled onward. Then they halted to listen.

"I don't know whether I'm any good at judging distances," Dick whispered, "but it seemed to me that whatever exploded was not much more than three hundred yards from camp."

"About that distance, I should say," Tom agreed.

"Then we've gone about as far as the place of the explosion. Suppose we keep very quiet and listen."

"Ugh!" grunted Greg. "I hope the earth doesn't blow up under our feet."

"Go back to camp, if you're nervous," smiled Dick, but Greg remained where he was.

"I'm going out a little way and prowl," whispered Dick, pointing in the direction he had chosen. "Tom, why don't you travel in about the opposite direction?"

Reade nodded.

"Where shall I go?" asked Greg.

"You had better remain right here," Prescott whispered. "If you should hear either of us yell for help then you could start in the direction of the sound."

"Then I'll get into those bushes," whispered Greg. "When you come back, come straight to the bushes, so I'll know that it's one of my own crowd. If any strangers appear, I'll listen to 'em if they halt near here, or trail them if they try to go past here."

Dick nodded. This seemed about the best that could be done. Of course, back in camp, he had three more good and courageous fellows to draw upon as added forces, but with such strange doings afoot in the night it didn't seem wise to call the others away from the camp. Above all, the camp had to be watched and guarded.

In half an hour Dick returned. He had found nothing to throw light on the puzzle of the night. Tom was back already, having beaten Dick to Greg's hiding place by about two minutes.

"We may as well go back to camp," whispered Greg.

"Not much!" Prescott retorted. "If anyone is trying to do anything to us, then we want to run the mystery down and put an end to it. My idea is that the best thing we can do is to get up to the road, post ourselves at fair intervals and watch to see if anyone should pass."

"Correct!" clicked Reade. "And I think that would have been the best plan in the first instance."

"If the powder-mill explosions are to keep up through the night," hinted Tom, "then there ought to be another one due within a few minutes. In that case our tormentors may be getting ready to plan something now. So let's hike for the road at once."

Dick led the way, all three boys moving as noiselessly as they could. Prescott posted his friends, then chose his own post, so that they were stationed at intervals of about a hundred yards. All had hiding places within plain view of this rough country road.

Now the time dragged again. Strain their ears as they might, none of these young outposts of Dick & Co. could hear a single suspicious sound. They must have remained there all of three quarters of an hour.

Bang! sounded a terrific crash. Tom and Greg, without showing themselves in the road, hurriedly, silently reached their leader.

"Pshaw!" uttered Prescott in disgust. "With all our care we were on the wrong side of camp to be near the explosion. Come along, now, but don't make any noise if you can help it, and don't step out into the road. We'll go straight toward that latest noise. If it takes all summer we're simply bound to find out who is trying to blow up these woods just to scare out a few little rabbits like ourselves!"

# CHAPTER XI
## IN A FEVER "TO FIND OUT"

Our trio had nearly reached what they judged to be the scene of the latest explosion when Dick suddenly gave a low, sharp "hist," at the same time bending over to the ground while still peering ahead.

Palpitating with excitement, Tom and Greg halted, also looking.

Out of the shadow ahead emerged something only vaguely outlined in the dark. Whether wild animal or human being it would be hard to say there in the darkness. Indeed, the slight sound caused by its progress close to the road had more to do with warning Dick and his friends than anything their eyes saw at first.

"Come on!" whispered Dick, heading suddenly for the road. In a jiffy Tom and Greg were also in hot pursuit, though young Prescott managed to keep somewhat in the lead.

But the object of their pursuit took alarm, too, and gaining the road, flew like the wind.

"Hold on there, you!" challenged Dick. "We want a little conversation with you at once."

At that vocal warning the fugitive put on an even better burst of speed.

"It must be a man!" exclaimed Dick. "He evidently understood me."

"No use for you to try to get away!" shouted Reade. "We intend to get you if we have to chase you all the way to the seaboard."

That was enough to make the fugitive veer suddenly and dart in under the trees. Tom vented an exclamation of disappointment, for he knew the chances were easy for escape in the deep shadows of the forest.

At that instant Dick raised his right hand. In it he held a small stone that he had picked up at the first instant of discovering the presence of the stranger.

Now Dick threw the stone, with the best judgment that he could command in the darkness.

Ahead there went up a cry, as though of pain. Then all three pursuers distinctly heard an angry voice say!

"Hang him! He hit me in the heel!"

If there were any reply to this from a confederate of the injured fugitive neither Dick nor his chums heard it.

After a minute all three stopped at a low uttered order from young Prescott.

"Hush!" whispered Dick.

"Sh!" confirmed Tom Reade.

As they stood there in the forest not a sound of another human being was audible.

For some five minutes the trio of high school boys stood without stirring from their tracks.

"We've lost the trail," whispered Dick at last. "We could remain here, of course, waiting for more things to happen, but my belief is that daylight would find us still standing here, like so many foiled dummies. We might as well return to camp. What do you think?"

"Yes; we'd better go back to camp," assented Tom.

"I'm agreeable," murmured Greg

So back to camp they went, going by the open road as much of the way as served their purpose.

"There's the camp," muttered Tom, as they caught sight of a light between the trees. "Why the fellows have started a campfire."

"What do you say if we slip up on them and give them something to jump about?" laughed Greg.

"That might work with some people," negatived Dick, "but Darry is there, and he's impulsive. He might half kill us before he discovered his mistake. O-o-o-h, Dave!"

"Hello!" answered Darrin, coming away from the campfire. Then he waited until the trio were close at hand before he went on:

"I judge you didn't have any luck."

"We got close to one of the scamps," muttered Tom, "whom Dick seems to have hit on the heel with a stone, but he slipped away from us under the trees."

"It's only half an hour to dawn," yawned Dave, looking at his watch. "We can turn in, now, I guess, for the rascals must be about through with the guessing match they've put up for us."

"We could turn in now," suggested Danny Grin. "We don't have to go to sleep, you know, but we could lie in our blankets and talk the time away until dawn. The campfire will keep going until after daylight comes on."

That seemed rather a sensible course. Dick nodded, and all hands, after Darry had thrown a few more sticks on the fire, went into the tent, undressed, donned pajamas and slipped in under a single thickness of blanket apiece, and lay there talking.

Yet it proved to be a case of gape and yawn. One after another their eyes closed and more regular breathing started.

Dick Prescott was the last one to drop off. Yet he had barely more than lost himself in slumberland when there came a blast so close at hand that, to the boys, it seemed as though they must have been blown from their cots.

"That was right up toward the road!" panted Dave Darrin, leaping from his cot barefooted and clad only in pajamas. "Don't stop to dress. Come on! Chase 'em!"

"Go as far as you like!" chuckled Dick, stopping to pull on his shoes and fasten them, as did most of the others. Hazelton went only to the doorway of the tent, but Danny Grin followed Darrin, keeping at the latter's heels.

Prescott and Reade were hardly sixty seconds later in heading up the slope toward the road, Greg and Harry remaining at the camp.

As they came out from under the trees and into the road Dick discovered that the first signs of dawn were appearing. In a few minutes more it would be possible to see clearly over a stretch of road more than half a mile in length. Already objects were beginning to take shape. Dave was coming back, followed by Dan. Both were limping slightly, for neither boy was accustomed to traveling barefoot and both had picked up slight stone bruises in their progress.

"Did you sight anything or anyone?" called Dick.

"No," grumbled Darrin, in deep disgust. "The odds are all against us, anyway. The scoundrels know which way they are going; we can only guess at their course."

"One thing looks rather certain, at any rate," yawned Dick, covering his mouth with his hand. "Whoever the unknowns are, they were trying only to bother us. Or, if they were trying to injure us, they were rank amateurs at the destructive game.

"But what was it that blew up, anyway?" queried Dave.

"It sounded like a keg of gunpowder each time," Tom declared. "Yet to carry around five kegs of gunpowder would call for a lot of muscular work."

"I'm going back to camp to put on my shoes," Dave declared.

"So am I," Danny Grin added.

"We'll wait here for you," said Dick. "When you come back there may be light enough for us to look into matters a little."

Dave and Dan returned in a little more than five minutes afterwards. The daylight was now becoming stronger.

"Are Greg and Harry keeping awake?" was Prescott's first question.

"They are," nodded Darrin.

"Then they can be trusted to look after the camp," Dick continued.

"And to look after the canoe," Reade amended.

"Now, we'll explore the woods a bit," Prescott went on. "We know about where we heard the explosions, and we'll look for whatever evidence we can find."

For this purpose each explorer went by himself. Ten minutes later Dave Darrin set up a loud hello. This brought the others to him on the run.

"Give us another call," demanded Dick.

"Here!" called Dave, from the depths of the woods.

Dick went in, followed by Tom and Dan.

"I've found this much," Dave announced, holding up a scorched bit of colored paper. It was such paper as is used for the outer wrapping of fireworks.

Dick took the fragment of paper, reading therefrom the title, "The Sploderite Pyrotechnic Co."

"Nothing but fireworks, after all," ejaculated Danny Grin in great contempt, now that it was broad daylight.

"But I would like to have seen the fireworks before they blew up," retorted Tom Reade. "They were surely the loudest I ever heard. I don't believe anything but the heaviest cannon could make as much noise."

"Whoever touched off fireworks like these," uttered Dave, "didn't care a hang whether or not he set the woods on fire."

"There was no fire danger," Dick rejoined. "The grass and everything in these forests is as green as can be. But let's look about and see if we can't find evidences of the explosion at this point."

"There ought to be a good-sized hole in the ground right under where this piece of fireworks exploded," Tom guessed. "We ought to find, not far from here, some evidences of what explosives can do in ripping up the ground."

"Now I remember that one of the explosions in the night sent something whizzing through the air over our heads."

"Pieces of the pasteboard enclosing the mine, bomb or whatever kind of fireworks it was," Dick suggested. "But let's look for other debris around here."

That single bit of scorched paper, however, was all that any of them could find.

Tom discovered a spot where he thought the ground had been blackened, but Dave thought the blackened appearance due to humus soil, and so nothing came of the argument.

"I think," yawned Dick, "this search will lead to the same result that the others did during the night. About all we can do is to go back to camp."

The sun was up by the time that all six members of Dick & Co. were once more gathered about the remains of their campfire.

"I don't know what you fellows are going to do," yawned Tom Reade. "As for me, at present a nap looks better than any shower bath or breakfast that was ever invented. No matter how much objection I hear, I'm going to get an hour or two more of sleep."

That idea met with rather a hearty reception. Within three minutes all six high school boys were lying between blankets again, composed for sleep.

No more explosions came to disturb their slumbers, which were deep and broken only when at last Dick Prescott called out:

"Fellows, we're regular Rip Van Winkles! It's half-past nine o'clock!"

"And we've that lake mystery to solve today!" uttered Greg Holmes, leaping up.

---

## CHAPTER XII
## DICK MAKES A FIND

Now, I don't know how it is going to hit the rest of you," remarked Tom Reade, as he put down his coffee cup at the end of the hasty breakfast, "but I'll confess that I'm not wholly keen about solving the puzzle of the lake mystery."

"Why not?" challenged Dave in astonishment.

"It's just like this," Tom went on. "Solving human riddles is all right in the daytime, but it's likely to spoil our rest at night. I can't help feeling that last night's Sploderite function was a mark of displeasure over our unwelcome interest in the lake mystery."

"Suppose we grant that," Dick answered, "yet how would last night's rascals expect us to connect the bang concert with Tom and Dan's canoe trip and discovery yesterday afternoon?"

"There's something in that idea," Reade admitted. "The unknowns might hardly expect us to show as much human reasoning power as all that. Yet I'm of the opinion that we'll continue to rest badly at night as long as we continue to feel any unhealthy curiosity about the lake mystery. In other words, my belief is that our interest in the affairs of perfect strangers is regarded by the unknowns as rudeness that must be rebuked."

"I don't care a hang about the lake mystery, anyway," gaped Dan, who was giving forth a series of yawns, his mouth only partially hidden by his right hand.

"There's just one strong point to the other side of the question," Dick argued. "There's a very fair amount of reason to believe that a man may have been drowned late yesterday afternoon, and that Tom and Dan saw him go down for the last time. That probability existing, I believe we are bound, as good citizens, to see if we can find any trace of a drowned man. If we can, then as good citizens it is clearly our further duty to report the matter to the authorities. If we can't find the remains of the drowned man, then I am under the impression that, at the least, Tom and Dan must report to some county officer just what they did see, and the county can then take up the question in any way it pleases. First of all, however, we ought to look for the body of a drowned man."

This view prevailing, Tom and Dan launched the canoe, Dick entering as passenger, while the other two handled the paddles.

Some brisk work took the canoe over, as nearly as Tom could judge, to the spot where the haunting face had been seen so briefly on the afternoon before.

Under the bright morning sun the waters were clear here, though the bottom could not be seen.

"Paddle half a mile up the lake, then down," Dick ordered.

This was done, Prescott and the paddlers keeping a sharp lookout. No body of a drowned man was seen, however, either on the surface or under the water.

"I don't believe anyone was drowned," re marked Dick at last. "There is no wind today, and hardly any such thing as current on this placid water. Whoever the man was, he got ashore."

"That's my belief," agreed Reade.

"Where's that brush arrangement?" asked Dan suddenly. "That frame all trimmed with green boughs."

Nor was this to be seen, either, though an object of that size would have been visible at any point on the water within half a mile.

"The man got ashore, all right, and he took care of the bush-trimmed frame as well," was Prescott's conclusion. "Whoever the man was, whatever happened, I don't believe that anything tragic happened in the water. For that matter, fellows, isn't it possible that, in the gathering gloom, and with the sky somewhat overcast, you were deceived about the ghastly, haunted look in that face? Isn't it likely that the look you thought you saw in the man's face was merely an effect of the unusual light of late yesterday afternoon?"

Tom shook his head emphatically.

"Why don't you ask us," demanded Dan ironically, "if it weren't just imagination on our part that we saw the face at all?"

"I don't doubt your having seen the face," Dick replied. "That wasn't anything that the light supplied."

"Then where is the man?" quizzed Dalzell.

"Safe on shore somewhere, beyond a doubt," Dick answered

"Then the chase takes us ashore, doesn't it?" asked Dan.

"Yes; if we're going to follow up the matter any further," Dick replied.

"We ought to follow it up," Reade insisted.

"Why?" asked Prescott.

"For one thing," smiled Tom, "it will give us something interesting to do."

"Should we find our interest in meddling with other folks' business?" wondered their leader.

"We've a right to, when those people come around and spoil our night's rest for us," Tom retorted.

"It was a bit like a challenge, wasn't it?" Dick laughed.

"Besides," Dan urged, "we certainly saw enough yesterday afternoon to show us that there is something tragic in the air around this sleepy old lake. If anyone is in trouble we ought to try to help that one out of trouble. And there was real, aching trouble in that face if ever I saw evidences of trouble."

"I guess we'll put in part of the day looking into the matter," Dick assented.

"Where shall we land?" asked Dalzell.

"As nearly as possible opposite the exact spot where you saw the man's head," Prescott made answer.

"Over there where that bent birch shows between the two chestnut trees," announced Reade, pointing with his paddle.

"Pull for that place," Dick ordered.

In a few minutes the canoe was drawn up along the shore so that Dick could step on land.

"You'd better come with me, Tom," said Prescott.

"And I'm the nifty little boat-tender who stays here and dozes in the shade?" asked Danny Grin, with a grimace.

"Are you good and strong this morning?" queried Dick, with a smile.

"Strong enough to walk, anyway," Dan retorted.

"Then perhaps you're strong enough to paddle back across the lake and bring over two more fellows. Then, when you get back here, leave one of the pair here in the canoe, and we will get them to keep it a hundred feet or more off shore. We don't want our craft destroyed. And be sure, Dan, that the fellow who stays behind on the other side of the lake understands that he's to stick right by the camp and watch it for all he's worth."

"I've got my orders," clicked Danny Grin, with a mock salute.

"Then let's see how well you can paddle alone."

Dalzell gave a few swift, strong turns of the paddle that sent the light canvas canoe darting over the water.

"Now, come along," urged Tom. "I'm anxious to get busy this morning."

First of all, the two high school boys walked up the lake shore for some distance, keeping their eyes wide open and all their senses on the alert. Then, returning, they walked for a considerable distance down the shore.

"There are our reinforcements coming," announced Tom, pointing across the lake. "Danny and his load will be here within fifteen minutes."

"We'll wait for the other fellows, before going away from the shore," Dick proposed. "If we started now they wouldn't know where to find us."

Returning to the landing place, Dick silently waved his hat until he caught the attention of Dave Darrin, seated in the bow of the canoe, who answered the signal just as silently.

Presently the craft came up to the shore.

"Who's going to stay in the canoe?" Dick inquired.

"I am," Harry Hazelton declared dolefully. "We drew lots on the other side. Greg drew the shortest twig, so he had to stay at the camp. I got the next shortest twig, so my job is boat-tender."

Dave and Dan stepped ashore. Heaving a sigh, Harry paddled out on the lake some hundred and fifty feet from land.

"Now, how are we going to beat up the country on this fine July morning?" Tom wanted to know.

Dick stood looking at the surrounding ground.

"I think I know as good a plan as any," he announced, after a pause. "Dave, you and I will walk down the lake, using our eyes and ears. Tom and Dan will go in the opposite direction. Each pair will keep along until our watches show that we've been going ten minutes. Then we will walk up the slope a hundred steps and turn toward the centre, meeting probably about the end of the second ten minutes. After that, if we decide to do so, we can go further inland from the lake. If there's a house or hut, or any fellow camping out in this neighborhood we ought to find him without much trouble. What do you fellows say to my plan?"

"It's about as systematic as anything could be," Dave agreed. "But what if one pair of us find something?"

"We'll try our best to communicate with the other pair," Dick rejoined. "Suppose, Dave, that you and I run into something interesting and don't want to leave it? Tom and Dan, not meeting us at the appointed place, will know enough to keep right on over our course until they find us."

"That looks plain enough," nodded Reade thoughtfully.

"All right, then," Dick declared. "Now we'll start."

He and Dave started off at a swinging gait. The first time Prescott turned to look behind him Reade and Danny Grin had already vanished.

Dick kept close to the shore, Dave moving in a parallel line a few steps up the slope.

"There isn't any hut, lodge or camp down there," Dave called softly, "or else we'd have seen it from our camp on the other side of the lake."

"I know it," Dick nodded. "What I'm trying to do is to see if I can find any hint, on the shore, of how that fellow landed yesterday, without Tom or Danny catching sight of him. Of course, a very clever swimmer could have gone quite a distance under water. and I want to see if I can find any sign of anything that would have hidden his landing from the fellows in the canoe."

"Oh!" nodded Dave understandingly.

The full ten minutes of searching passed without the slightest trace of a discovery.

"Halt," Dick called up smilingly. "Now, join me, Darry, while I count off the hundred steps up the slope."

This done, the chums started backward, keeping a course as nearly parallel with the shore as was possible.

"Now, try to be keener than ever," Dick urged, as Dave paced off another twenty steps higher up. "We're in a growth of deeper forest, with a bigger tangle of underbrush and it will be easy enough to overlook something."

The two boys trudged on. They were five minutes on their way back, perhaps, when Dick heard a sudden scrambling in the underbrush not far away. Then Prescott caught sight of a human figure, yet so fleetingly that he could have given no description of it.

"Is that you, Darry?" he called sharply.

But it wasn't, for no answer came back, save for the slight sound of someone going through the brush farther on.

"Dave! Darry!" shouted Prescott. "Here! Quickly!"

Then Dick dashed on in pursuit, calling again and again until Dave came in sight and joined in the chase.

"What was it?" panted Dave, as he came within hailing distance.

"Someone running away from me," Dick explained.

"What did he look like?"

"I didn't have a chance to see. Let's travel hot-foot."

Yet presently Dick halted. Dave stopped beside him.

"We've passed him; he has doubled on us," uttered Darrin in a tone of intense chagrin. "We belong in the primary class in wood lore."

Then, suddenly, they heard a slight noise again. Forward they dashed. Now they came out to a place where the ground was more open. Before the two high school boys rose a great boulder of rock, its front sloping backward, and running up to a height of fifty feet or more. They had already seen this boulder from the water.

"That fellow ran into the open, but he didn't have time to cross it," announced Dick in a tone of conviction, as the pair halted at the foot of the boulder. "He could have gone up this side; there are crevices enough for foothold. But in that case we'd have seen him." Dave stood plucking absent-mindedly at the leaves of a bush in a clump that grew at the foot of the boulder. Suddenly Dick glanced down, noting that his feet were on boggy ground, though the surrounding soil was firm enough.

"Is there a spring running out of the solid rock?" wondered Dick, reaching out and pulling one of the bushes forward.

Then he gave a sudden shout of discovery:

"Look here, Dave! We're on the track of it! These bushes conceal the mouth of a cave! This is where our fugitive has gone!"

## CHAPTER XIII
## PERHAPS TEN THOUSAND YEARS OLD

By Jove!" gasped Dave, also bending back a bush and glaring down, his eyes wide open with interest.

"That's where our man went," Dick whispered.

"Not a doubt of it," Dave assented. "We'll signal the other fellows, and then get him at our leisure."

"Unless there are other openings to this cave," Dick hinted.

"That's so! The fellow may be a quarter of a mile away from here already," Darrin quivered. "Let's not lose any time. I'll go in there first."

Dave was on his knees, quivering with eagerness, dominated by purpose, when Dick grabbed him, hauling him back.

"Let me alone," growled Dave. "Don't interfere with me!"

"But you don't know what you might run into in there, Darry," Prescott insisted firmly. "For one thing, you have no idea how many villains may have their secret home in there."

"Then, what are you going to do?" Darry demanded, looking up.

"I'm going to watch, right here, while you go forward and find Tom and Dan. Bring them here, and then we'll decide what ought to be done."

"That's rather slow," hot-headed Darry objected.

"It is, and a heap safer," Dick contended. "Hot-foot it after Tom and Dan. I'll stay right here and see to it that the mouth of the cave doesn't run away. Start---at once, Darry, please! Don't let us waste time."

Knowing how stubborn Dick could be when he knew that he was wholly right, Dave lost no time in argument. He sprinted away, and presently Dick heard faint echoes of Darry's signaling, "hoo-hoo!"

A few minutes later the trio came up at a dog trot.

Not one of them spoke, as all had lost their breath in their haste. Tom, now in the lead, dashed up to where Dick stood on guard a few yards away from the bushes.

"Over there," nodded Dick, pointing to the bushes.

Tom and Dan pulled the bushes aside curiously.

"If we're going into that cave we may as well cut the bushes down," murmured Reade, producing a pocket knife. "Any objections, Chief?"

"No," smiled Dick, "and I'm not the Big Chief, either. Cut the bushes down, if you want. Move over, and I'll give you some help."

Within a short time the bushes had been cut down close to the ground, revealing an irregular shaped opening in the cave. This aperture was about three feet high and some five feet in width.

"Did you bring that pocket flash lamp, Tom?" asked Dick suddenly.

"Thank goodness, I did," replied Reade, producing the lamp.

Dick took it and crawled a few feet into the hole.

"There's water all along on the floor here," he called, "but just a dribble. Come in here and you'll find that you can stand up."

It needed no urging to induce the other boys to follow. Then they stood up, in almost complete darkness, save when the flashlight showed them their surroundings.

Some parts of the cave rose to a height of perhaps sixteen feet. Twelve feet was about the average height. From what the boys could see as they moved along, the cave extended for some sixty feet.

"I don't believe there's anyone in here except ourselves," muttered Darry in disgust, peering all around him. "In that case, we are wasting our time in this cave. Phew! How cold it is in here!"

"And well it might be," laughed Dick. "Do you see that mass just ahead of us?"

"What is it?" asked Dan. "Flash the light on it."

"Come over and look at it," Dick went on. "No one could live in this cold place. It is chilling me to the bone, just to stand here. And now you see why that little trickle of water keeps moving out through the mouth of the cave. Fellows, we're in one of nature's icehouses."

"But we're not after ice," Dave protested.

"We won't turn down ice in the wilderness, when we can find it in July," Dick rejoined.

"Not much!" answered practical Tom Reade. "Why, fellows, ice is just what we need at the camp. Let's get a closer look at it and make plans for an ice-box over at the camp."

"But I want to follow that man of mystery," protested Dave.

"Go ahead, David, little giant," Dick laughed. "We won't stop you. But we've lost our man of mystery, anyway, and this cave contains something that we really do want. Tom, you're the mathematician of the party. How much ice is there here?"

"If I could see better I could tell you better," sniffed Reade. "Hundreds of tons of it, anyway."

"How did the stuff get here?" asked Dan wonderingly.

Dick was now at the edge of the ice pile, and flashed the light at the roof of the cavern.

"See the rifts in the rock up there?" he asked. "Water must have leaked in here during the heavy winter rains. It was cold water, too. Then, in extra cold spells, such as this country experiences, the water must have frozen. As heat doesn't get in here in warm weather the ice may have been here for generations. Fellows, we may be looking upon ice that was here when George Washington was a boy."

"I've read, somewhere," declared Tom soberly, "that icebergs that float down from the polar regions in spring often represent ice that is at least ten thousand years old. Fellows, some of this very ice may have been here in this cave long, long before Julius Caesar went into the soldiering business!"

That thought had somewhat of an awesome effect upon Dick & Co. The four high school boys felt as though they were in the presence of great antiquity.

"But the practical side of it," declared Tom, "is that we must devise the best way of cutting some of this ice and getting it across the lake to the camp."

"Oh, you can break off enough for making ice water," replied Dave Darrin impatiently, "and take it over in the canoe, though the spring water is cold enough for anybody."

"All of Dave's thoughts are still on the man of mystery," Dick declared, with a chuckle.

"It's much more interesting than standing here figuring on how to get ice that we don't need," retorted Darry.

"Now, as to moving this stuff to the camp," Tom went on, "it seems to me-----"

"Of course," laughed Dick. "It has already struck you that we can fell a few small trees and build a raft on which we can tow a few hundred pounds of ice at a time."

"Oh, pshaw!" fidgeted Dave. "I am anxious to find the man of mystery."

"That isn't anything practical," scoffed Tom Reade, "while in hot weather a good supply of ice is eminently practical."

"You'll think there's a practical side to the man of mystery and his cronies when to-night comes, and there's so much noise about the camp that we miss another night's rest," hinted Darry sagely.

"Humph!" was Tom's greeting to that assertion. "I don't know but you're right."

"Well, we know where the ice is," remarked Dick. "We can get it at our convenience. Darry, we'll follow you in pursuit of your man of mystery. Come out of here, fellows."

Dick led the way out of the cave, flashing the light as he walked. All four blinked when they found themselves out in the sunlight.

"Now, which way are we going, David, little giant?" demanded Tom good-humoredly.

Now that he was put to it, Dave had to confess that he didn't know.

"Let's make a swift, thorough search all around here, and see if we can find any footprints not made by ourselves," Dave suggested rather weakly, at last.

This was done, and faithfully, for, now that they were out in the sunlight again, the interest in the mystery began to return. It grew stronger as they searched. At last, however, after more than an hour of fruitless effort that offered not an atom of promise, even Darry was willing to give it up for the time, at any rate.

"Let's keep on walking along the slope, then," Dick suggested, "until we come in sight of the canoe."

As they walked along they came to a brook that, at this point, was nearly the width of a creek. The water ran noisily down over the stones, save here and there where there were deep pools.

"It's narrow enough, at one point below here, to jump over," Dave volunteered.

"Thank you," replied Dick, "but just at present I'm not for jumping over this brook."

"Well, then, what on earth does interest you?" Dan asked. "This isn't the first time you've seen this stream. You passed it down by the lake, though down there it runs more smoothly."

"I know," Dick nodded. "I remember the fallen tree we used for a bridge, and I'm simply ashamed of myself that I didn't think more about this stream at the time---but my head was then too full of the lake mystery and the chap with the haunting face. But now-----"

"Well?" demanded Tom impatiently.

"Reade, old fellow," Dick answered solemnly, turning back from peering at one of the quiet pools in the creek, "you're a wonder at black bass fishing, no doubt. My tastes ran to another form of sport. Mr. Morton taught me trout fishing; he lent me his tackle before we started, and I have it over at the camp now. Fellows, I believe, from the looks of things, that this stream is well stocked with trout. At all events, I mean to have a try at it."

"To-morrow?" asked Dave.

"No, siree! This afternoon----just as soon as possible! A little while ago we were talking about ferrying ice over to the camp. Instead, we'll ferry the camp over here, and keep the cave just as it is for our ice-house. Do you fellows know that brook trout make the most delicious eating to be had when the cook knows his business? I do, for Mr. Morton has cooked trout for me in the woods. Besides, brook trout are growing scarce these days. If we can make a good haul, we can get a pretty big price per pound for them! We have ice, now, and we could carry a lot of trout to market on our push cart, on top of enough ice to keep them. Come on! Back to camp! We'll shift it to this side of the lake at once. This crowd can't do better than to work out this trout stream. I know the trout are there! I can smell 'em! Tom, I've got an important job for you!"

## CHAPTER XIV
## MORE MYSTERY IN THE AIR

It was nearly dark, after an afternoon of hard work for five members of the party, and an afternoon of wonderful sport for Dick Prescott.

A crude raft had been built. That part of the work had been easy, and it was swiftly performed. But three trips with the small raft had been needed to bring over the tent, the supplies, the push cart and everything belonging to the old camp.

Now the new camp stood pitched at a short distance from the cave, but near to the edge of the lake. The tent had been put up in a natural clearing, behind a line of timber, so that the canvas was not visible from the other side of the lake.

At trout fishing Dick had proved himself more than an expert.

Now that darkness was coming, Dick was bending over a low fire, watching a frying pan in which four speckled beauties, well dipped in batter, were sizzling merrily.

"This is the finest food I've ever had," declared Greg Holmes, swallowing another mouthful of trout and leaning back with a contented sigh.

"It certainly is great," agreed Dave Darrin. "Fellows, I've wasted some of my life in the past, for I never before knew the taste of brook trout."

"I tried 'em once," said Reade, "but they didn't taste as fine as these. With trout, I've heard, a tremendous lot depends upon the way they're cooked."

"Of course the cooking has a lot to do with bringing out the full flavor," Dick admitted modestly. "But, Tom, perhaps you hadn't done any hard work before eating trout that time. Exercise brings hunger, and hunger is the best sauce that food can have---as we all ought to know."

"Exercise?" repeated Tom, with a laugh. "Yes; I've had that this afternoon, all right.  You had me guessing when you told me you had such an important job for me.  I didn't know, then, that you wanted me to boss the raft building and transporting the camp over here.  It was exercise, all right.  We ought to have taken an entire day to it."

Dick rose with the frying pan, dropping hot trout on four plates in turn, omitting only Holmes.

"You shall have a trout out of the next serving, Greg," Dick promised.

"I'm not worrying about myself," Greg returned.  "But are you going to have anything left for yourself, Dick?"

"I'm not worrying about that, either," laughed Prescott.  "It was mighty nice of you fellows to do all the work this afternoon, and leave me to enjoy myself all the time at sport.  So the trout belong to you fellows."

"I don't suppose you worked at all, Dick," said Tom quizzically.  "Of course whipping up and down a stream in rubber boots, over stones and all sorts of obstacles, isn't anything like work."

"It would be pretty hard work for a fellow who didn't like trout fishing, I suppose," Dick answered.  "But, to me, it was only so much glorious sport.  Here's your trout, Greg.  Who else wants some more?"

"Don't ask foolish questions," chuckled Danny Grin.

But at last the five boys had to admit that they had eaten their fill out of the splendid result of Dick's afternoon of sport.  There were still several trout left, all cleaned and ready to be dipped in the batter.

"Now, you sit down at the table, and let us wait on you," urged Greg, going over to Dick.

Dave took hold of one of young Holmes' suspender straps, pulling him back.

"You simpleton," expostulated Darry, "are you going to spoil Dick's reward by letting a chump cook attend to the trout?  Dick wants to cook his trout for himself, but we'll do everything else. I'll appoint myself to make the coffee for all hands."

Dick soon had a pan full of trout ready for his own plate.  As he seated himself at the table he was fully conscious of how tired and sore he was from the afternoon of whipping up and down stream after these handsome, speckled fish, but he was careful not to admit his fatigue to the others, who, also, were very tired.

Dick had to fry a second pan of trout, eating the last one of the lot he had caught, ere he found his appetite satisfied.

Then, with only the light of a lantern on the table, the boys sat about sipping their coffee and feeling supremely contented with their day of effort and its results.

"There are not so many mosquitoes over here," Tom announced.

"They haven't found us out yet," chuckled Danny Grin. "They will do so, later."

"I'm ready for bed any time the word comes," confessed Harry Hazelton.

"But, see here, fellows," suggested Dave soberly, "we're now right in the enemy's country. That is to say, we're on the same side of the lake with the man of mystery and his companions, if he has any. I don't doubt that resentful eyes have watched the erecting of this camp on its present site."

"Sorry to have hurt anyone's feelings," yawned Tom. "Still, I guess we've as much right here as anyone else."

"But the point is this," Dave went on. "Last night some persons must have crossed the lake in order to annoy us. To-night we're on the same side of the lake with them. We'll be much more accessible to the people who object so strenuously to our presence."

"Where did these unknown people find a boat for crossing the lake?" queried Reade. "We couldn't find one anywhere until the canoe was left at our camp."

"Anyone might have a boat or canoe here, and keep it hidden easily enough when not in use," Dave asserted. "Just as we---have brought our canoe up here and hidden it in the tent, for instance. Now, we'll all have to admit that we're extremely likely to have unwelcome visitors here to-night? Are we going to keep a guard?"

"It might not be a bad idea to keep someone on watch through the night," Dick suggested.

"I'll stand the first watch trick," proposed Dave. "It need be only an hour long. I'll drink some more coffee, and then walk a while, so as to be sure to keep awake."

"I'll take the second trick," nodded Dick.

The schedule for watch tricks was quickly made up. Then all but Dave hastily sought their cots. Darkness was not an hour old when Dave was the only member of the camp awake. Had the high school boys been less healthy and sturdy their hearty suppers might have summoned the nightmare, but they slept on soundly.

Dick, however, stretched, gaped, then sprang up when Darry called him. Some of the others, when their turns came, did not respond as readily, and had to be dragged from their cots and stood upright before they were thoroughly awake.

It was shortly after one o'clock in the morning when Tom Reade, then on watch, stepped lightly into the tent, passing through the round of the cots, shaking each sleeper in turn. "Those of you who want to listen to something interesting, get up instantly!" Tom exclaimed in a low voice.

Three boys drowsily rolled over, going immediately back into sound slumber. Dick and Dave, however, got up, pulling on their shoes.

"What's all that racket across the lake?" was Dick's prompt question as he stood in the doorway of the tent.

"That comes from the former camp site," chuckled Tom.

"Guns!" cried Dave Darrin in amazement.

"It sounds like a big fusillade," Dick cried, as he stepped out into the night.

"But surely no one can be trying to attack our camp, thinking we are still there," Tom protested. "We don't know any people who are wicked enough to plan an attack upon our camp."

"No," Dick agreed. "But this much is sure. There are those who dislike us enough to try to spoil our rest night after night."

Dave began to laugh merrily.

"I half believe it's Dodge and Bayliss," he remarked quietly.

"I don't," Reade objected. "Both of them are too lazy to motor up into the wilderness each night, over such rough roads, all the way from Gridley. No, no! It's someone else, though who it is I can't imagine. If it were the man of the lake mystery, or any of his people, they'd be likely to know that we're on this side of the lake." From the edge of the timber line near by came the sound of a crackling twig, followed by a groan as of a soul in torment.

Wheeling like a flash, Tom Reade produced the pocket flash lamp.

Staring toward the boys, his face outlined between the close-growing trunks of two spruce trees, were the startling features of a man.

"That's he---the Man of the Haunting Face!" came from Tom Reade in a hoarse whisper.

"Then we'll get him!" cried Dick Prescott, leaping forward. "Hold the light on him!"

## CHAPTER XV
## THE SCREAM THAT STARTED A RACE

Yet even as the three boys dashed toward the two spruce trees the light went out.

Tom pressed frantically on the spring of the lamp as he ran, but the lamp gave forth a flickering gleam that was little better than no light at all.

The long use of the lamp in the cave had weakened the storage battery.

"Give us the light!" called Dave, as they reached the tree.

"Can't! The battery's on a strike," answered Reade grimly.

Dick Prescott, who was ahead of his companions, now halted, whispering to the others to do the same.

The man they sought had vanished. No betraying sounds came to indicate where he had gone.

"Dave and I'll stay here," whispered Dick. "Tom, run back for a lantern. Hustle!"

Fifteen minutes of eager searching, after the lantern was brought, failed to give any clue to the whereabouts of the man whom they sought.

"This is more ghostly than human," laughed young Prescott.

They felt compelled to give up the search. As they returned to the camp the firing on the opposite side of the lake broke out anew. At the distance, however, it was not loud enough to disturb the other three, who still slept in the tent. Dick flashed the lantern inside to make sure that the sleepers were safe.

At intervals the racket across the lake broke out anew.

"It's my turn to go on watch again," said Darry, glancing at his watch by the light of the lantern. "You two might as well turn in."

"We'll dress and bring our cots out into the open," Dick proposed. "You might as well have us, Dave, where you can get us instantly, and ready for action, by just touching us on the shoulder."

But the night passed, without any further disturbances than the occasional distant firing, and the rousing, every hour, of a new watchman for the camp.

It was past seven in the morning when Dick finally turned out, to find Greg and Harry busy preparing breakfast, while Darrin still slumbered.

"Where are Tom and Dan?" Prescott asked.

"Look through the trees, and presently you'll discover them out in the canoe," answered Greg. "Tom simply couldn't wait any longer to go out after bass."

"I'm going trout fishing, if I can do it without shirking," said Dick, as he rose and stretched.

"And if no one kicks I'm going with you," added Darrin, opening his eyes. "How about it, Greg? Are you and Harry willing to do the camp watch this morning?"

Greg had turned around eagerly, seeing which, Hazelton broke in:

"Go right along with 'em, Holmesy, if they'll take you. There won't be much to do in camp after, the dishes are washed."

"But it's rather a shame to leave you alone," hinted Greg wistfully. He wanted, with all his heart, to see some of the rare sport that Dick had described, but he didn't want to be unfair to anyone.

"I won't be lonesome," protested Hazelton. "We have some good books along, and I can read one of them."

"But what if the camp should be molested?" asked Greg. "You know, there is at least the Man with the Haunting Face, and there may be others."

"Whoever tries to molest this camp will be molested in his turn, I promise you," laughed Harry. "I'm no weakling, so run right along, Holmesy. Even if serious trouble should arise, I have this, you know."

He produced a long-barreled fish horn that he had used in celebrating the night before the Fourth of July.

"Two or three loud blasts on this bugle would carry a long way, and you fellows would know what I wanted," finished Hazelton.

"All right, then, I'll go," said Greg, his face beaming.

"We've trout flies in plenty, you know," Dick went on, "but we've only two poles that are suited to trouting, so we'll have to take turns."

"You may keep one pole all the time. Dick," suggested Darry. "Greg and I can take turns with the other pole."

"That will hardly be fair to you two," replied Dick, with a shake of his head.

"It wouldn't be fair to the whole crowd to take your pole away from you any part of the time," retorted Greg. "Remember, Dick, you are the expert trout fisherman of the party, and all the fellows want some more trout. We'll never forget those of last night."

Greg and Hazelton now had breakfast ready. It was eaten rather hastily, after which all hands fell to setting things to rights.

"Here, come out of the tent," called Hazelton, as Dick started inside to use a broom there. "You fellows are the providers, and I can do the little housework that's left to do."

So Dick, Dave and Greg brought out their long-legged rubber boots and got into them with little delay. Then there came a sorting of flies, and the rigging of lines and reels. Within a few minutes the three were ready to start out.

As they went up the stream Dick cut and trimmed two crotched sticks on which to string the fish they might catch.

"That looks almost boastful," chuckled Dave. "It looks as though we thought it a cinch that we're going to get a lot of trout."

"It all depends on us," Prescott rejoined. "The brook is simply full of trout, that we can catch if we display the requisite amount of skill. The mystery to me is that this brook has escaped the knowledge of the trout fishermen in Gridley. Not even Mr. Morton ever heard of this stream."

"Well, Mr. Morton can't be expected to know everything," argued Greg. "He's already the most capable sub-master in Gridley High School and the finest coach the Gridley football squad ever had."

"He's also an A No. 1 trout fisherman," Dick went on. "Fellows, we mustn't tell everyone about this trout stream, but Mr. Morton is such an all around fine fellow that I think we owe it to him to tell him, when we see him, just how to reach this brook."

"If the real estate men of Gridley knew of this place," laughed Greg, "they'd buy up the ground around here and then sell bungalows at fancy prices to amateur fishermen of means."

"And then the brook would soon cease to be a trout stream," retorted young Prescott. "A large proportion of the trout would be caught within a few days, and the rest of 'em scared away to safer breeding grounds. The only way to keep a trout stream in working order is not to let many people know about it. It sounds selfish, but it's good sportsmanship."

Dick soon halted, eyeing a pool so deep that its bottom could not be seen.

"This looks like a good place to start in," he announced. "I believe I'll go a little way up stream, and then whip down past this pool and below. Now, talk only in whispers, if you can remember, fellows. Trout are shy creatures. Has either of you ever fished for trout before?"

Both Dave and Greg shook their heads.

"Then I think you had better watch me for a while, and catch some of the knack of it," their leader advised. "Notice particularly how I whip. If I get a nibble, then note, particularly, that I don't make an immediate effort to land the trout. I play the line out a bit and let him play with the fly, and beat about and get himself better imbedded on the hook. When I am sure I have him well hooked, then you'll see the peculiar motion with which I bring him out of the water and throw him on the ground. That landing trick is one that you need to get just so. Study it, and develop it. Don't be disappointed if you lose quite a few trout. You will lose them often until you get the hang of the thing."

Some distance above the pool Dick stepped into the water. He walked along slowly, not stirring up much dirt from the bottom. All the time he kept his line behind him, frequently lifting it and whipping it into the water again. The gayly colored flies and the glistening spoon just above the hook flashed in the sunlight every time he made a whipping cast.

Not twenty feet had Dick gone when he felt a sudden, violent tug. With the true patience of the trout fisherman, Dick didn't become at all excited. His hand on the reel, he let the line fly out as the finny captive darted up stream.

Presently Dick played the fish in gently, then suddenly gave it plenty of slack line. These tactics were repeated, while Dave and Greg almost danced in their eagerness.

Suddenly Dick flipped his pole sharply. There was a swish of line in the air.

Something speckled and glistening dropped on the ground at least ten feet from the brook, where it lay floundering and gasping.

"Hoo-ray!" yelled Greg, with all his pent-up enthusiasm.

"Do that again, Holmesy, and I'll chase you back into camp," warned Dick, with his patient smile.  Then he stepped ashore, took the trout from the line and impaled it on a stick, which he gave Greg to carry.

Within two minutes there was another strike.  The same patient tactics, and Dick had another trout---this time a two-pounder as against about three quarters of a pound for the weight of the first trout.

The third trout got away, despite the most careful handling, but the fourth and fifth biters were soon landed.

"I can't stand this any longer," quivered Dave.  "I've got to start in.  Where do you want me to go, Dick?"

"Better go about a quarter of a mile upstream," Prescott suggested, "and then work down this way.  Greg can go along with you and carry the stick for your string.  I'll look out for my own string."

For nearly half an hour Prescott saw nothing of his friends. Then Dave and Greg came in sight.  Dick held up a string now numbering eleven trout, some of them unusually large. For answer Greg held up a crotched stick with not a single trout dangling therefrom.

"There's more knack to this game than I can catch," muttered Darry disconsolately, "but I'd give a good deal to get the knack of it."

"No man save the first trout fisherman of all ever learned without a teacher," Dick assured his chum.  "Greg, you take a place farther down the stream, and I'll stay with Dave and try to show him some of the tricks.  You may have my pole and line, Greg, for I shall be busy watching Dave."

Many a pull at his line had Darrin, and many a fish was lost ere, under Prescott's patient instruction, he managed to land a trout weighing about a pound.

"Whew!" muttered Dave, mopping his brow. "At this moment I believe I feel prouder than any general who ever captured a city."

"You'll soon have the hang of it, now, Dave," was his chum's encouraging assurance.  "Now, I'm going to hunt up Holmesy, and see if I can show him some of the knack."

Greg proved a grateful though not very clever pupil. He was all enthusiasm, but the art of landing a trout appeared to him to be one of the most difficult feats in the world.

"I don't believe I'll ever land enough to fill a frying pan," he said dejectedly. "Dick, the fellows are depending upon you. Take this pole and use it for the next hour."

Later in the forenoon Greg had one small trout on a stick he had cut and trimmed for himself. Dave Darrin looked almost triumphant as he displayed three of the speckled ones. Both stared in envy at Dick's string of thirty-four trout.

"Of course it'll take a few days of patient study of the game to enable you to make big catches," was Dick's consoling assurance.

"I'd put in all summer, if I were sure I could master the trick in the end," said Dave. Greg said nothing, but felt less resolute about it than Darrin did.

"Why, it's only fifteen minutes before noon," cried Dave, glancing at his watch.

"Then it's high time to be going back," nodded Dick, "in case the fellows are depending upon us for their meal. If Tom has a lot of bass, though, we can store these trout in our new ice box---the cave."

"And let the Man with the Haunting Face slip in there, after dark, and help himself!" grumbled Darry. "Somehow that idea doesn't make any hit with me."

"Then we'll have to put in the afternoon," proposed Prescott, "in building a log-lined pit in the ground and moving ice from the cave to fill it. Then we can keep our fish supplies right up under our noses in front of the tent."

"That's a little more satisfactory in the way of an idea," nodded Darry.

For the purpose of taking a short cut they soon left the brook, going through a stretch of woods on their way to camp.

Hardly had these high school boys entered the woods when they halted, for an instant, in intense consternation.

On the air there came to them a sudden scream.

"That was a girl's voice!" gasped Greg.

"Or a woman's," nodded Dick. "We've got to-----"

Again a piercing scream, then more screams in two voices.

"Hustle!" finished Dick, as the three boys broke into a run in the direction whence the sound of the voices came to them.

# CHAPTER XVI
## THE CAMP INVADED AND CAPTURED

Clad in their long fishing boots, none of the boys made anything like his usual speed in running.

Grumbling inwardly at their clumsy gait, all three hurried as fast as they could into the near-by stretch of forest.

There, in a path, they came upon a middle-aged woman accompanied by four girls, all of whom showed signs of unusual alarm.

"Oh, Dave," called Belle Meade, "I'm so glad to see you!"

"You usually are," laughed Darrin, "but I never knew you to make so much noise about it before."

"What's the trouble?" Dick inquired, after a hasty greeting to Mrs. Bentley, Laura Bentley, Belle Meade, Fannie Upham and Margery White, the latter four all Gridley High School girls.

"A man---he must have been crazy!" replied Laura. Her voice shook slightly, and she was still trembling, though the color was beginning to return to her face.

"Did he offer to molest you?" flared Dick.

"No, indeed!" replied Mrs. Bentley promptly and laughing nervously. "In fact, I think we must have frightened the man, for his desire seemed to be to get away from us as fast as he could."

"But that face!" cried Miss Fanny. "I never want to see it again."

"It must have been our Man of the Haunting Face," murmured Dick, turning to his chums.

"That was he---just who it was!" declared Belle, with emphasis. "I don't know whom you're talking about, but 'haunting face' just describes the man who frightened us."

"It was so silly of us!" murmured Laura Bentley. "It was clear nonsense for us to be so frightened, but when, we saw that face peering at us from behind a tree we simply couldn't help screaming."

"Are you alone?" demanded Prescott in some astonishment, for these were carefully brought-up girls, and it was not like their parents to let them go into the woods without other guard than that of a chaperon.

At that instant Dick's question was answered by the appearance of Dr. Bentley, who, on account of his weight, panted somewhat as he ran.

"Did---these---young men frighten---you so badly---that you---made such a commotion---and caused me nearly to breathe---my last in running to---your aid?" demanded the good doctor gaspingly, his eyes twinkling.

"No, sir; we came, like yourself, when we heard the girls scream," Dick Prescott explained.

Then, amid much talking, and with as many as three people speaking at once, the story was quickly recounted for Dr. Bentley.

"We've seen the fellow before," Dick explained, "but he always fakes alarm and vanishes. We call him our man of mystery---the Man with the Haunting Face."

"Some poor, simple-minded fellow," suggested Dr. Bentley. "Probably one whose mild mania leads him to prefer to live in the woods, a regular hermit. My dears, I'm surprised that any of you should be so easily startled and make such noisy testimony to your alarm."

"I'm indignant with myself now---when there are men standing by," laughed Belle. "But I wish you had seen that man's strange face, Doctor."

"I would like to see it, and punch it, too!" muttered Dave.

"Not a bit of it!" objected Dr. Bentley heartily. "No doubt the poor fellow is sadly afflicted mentally. He's what the Arabs call a 'simple,' and the Arabs have a beautiful faith that all 'simples' are under the direct protection of Allah. So, woe to him who offends one of Allah's 'simples.'"

"How do you boys come to be here?" asked Laura.

"I might ask the same question of your party," smiled Dick. "As for us, we are away on a vacation fishing and camping trip."

"I knew you were going away," said Dr. Bentley, "but I didn't know just where. We are touring again, in my seven-passenger car. We are headed for the St. Clair

Lake House, eight miles below here. But the roads are so bad that the chauffeur said it would take us more than an hour to get through. So I proposed to Mrs. Bentley and the girls that we leave the car at the road and cross over here to have our luncheon on the shore of this second lake. I have been here before, and remember it as a beautiful spot. Mrs. Bentley and the girls started on ahead, and I brought up the rear with the baskets of food. But they got further ahead of me than I thought. Now I must go back after the baskets, which I set down before I started to run here. Greg, will you go back with me and help me bring the baskets?"

Greg at once accompanied the physician. When they came to the spot, however, they found but one basket, and that nearly empty. The second basket had disappeared altogether.

"Fine!" grunted Dr. Bentley. "Greg, our committee of two must go back and report the disquieting news."

"Not so very disquieting, sir," smiled young Holmes. "We have a camp full of food to offer you."

That invitation Dick and Dave very quickly seconded when the doctor rejoined the party.

"Especially if you can eat trout, sir," Dick went on.

"Don't! Don't be cruel!" remonstrated Dr. Bentley. "I used to eat trout when I was a boy, but they are now an extinct fish."

"Are they, sir?" inquired Dick, unwrapping a paper from around part of the morning's heavy catch, while Dave exhibited the contents of a similar bundle.

Dr. Bentley rubbed his eyes.

"Bless me, these are a fine imitation of brook trout as I recall them," he murmured.

"What did you mean by saying that trout were an extinct fish?" asked Laura.

"They're extinct for all but the wealthy," replied the physician. "Brook trout, in these days, generally cost all of a dollar and a half a pound, and I've heard of as high as two dollars a pound being paid for them."

"There are plenty hereabouts, just now," Dick replied. "But we may take them all out of the water before we move from here."

"Of course," nodded Laura's father. "That's what trout are for. They won't do anyone any good as long as they remain in the water."

"Let's hurry back, please," urged Dick. "I am anxious to see your luncheon under way."

"Yes," teased Belle, "the sooner you have satisfied our appetites the sooner you may expect to see us gone and be able to enjoy yourselves and your comfortable solitude once more."

"Now, just for saying that, Belle," uttered Dick reproachfully, "I'm going to consider the revenge of burning two of your trout in the pan."

"Mercy!" cried Belle Meade. "Are you going to cook the trout?"

"After you've eaten a trout cooked and served up by Dick Prescott," Dave declared, "you won't want them cooked by anyone else. Dick is the one trout chef in this part of the country."

"Where did he learn?" teased Belle with a pretense of suspicion.

"Mr. Morton---Coach Morton, of our high school eleven---taught Dick how to do it," Dave explained.

"Right here, young ladies---attention!" called Dr. Bentley, holding up a warning finger. "If brook trout are as fine eating as they used to be when I was a boy, then you simply won't be able to keep it a secret that you've eaten some recently. Yet on one point I must insist. None of you must be dishonorable enough to name any spot within fifty miles of here as the scene of your trout luncheon. If you let the secret out all the trout fishermen in four counties will be swarming here to destroy all the fun your young men friends are having. So, please remember! Utter, dark, uncompromising secrecy!"

"Is it as bad as that?" asked Belle.

"Every real trout fisherman knows enough to keep his own secrets as to the streams that contain trout," Dave nodded.

By this time they came within sight of the camp. Nor was it long before Tom, Dan and Harry caught sight of the visitors and ran forward to meet them.

"Our friends have come just in time to have a trout feast," Dick announced.

"I shall be jealous if they eat the trout," Tom retorted.

"Or envious?" laughed Belle.

"No; jealous," Tom assured her. "Dan and I have been fishing, too. Come and see what we caught."

Tom led the way to where he had cleaned more than a dozen black bass, while in buckets of water lay nearly thirty more fine, sleek-looking fish.

"Didn't you catch anything but bass?" Dave asked.

"A few other fish," Tom admitted, "but we threw the inferior fish back into the water. Now, girls, which are you going to have---trout or bass?"

"Both---if we may," ventured Laura, with a smile.

And both were served at the meal. Motherly Mrs. Bentley laid aside her motoring dust coat and marshaled the girls for the various tasks to which she assigned them.

What a hubbub there was in preparing the feast!

Dick built two small fires for his own exclusive use. Tom built two more, while Dan and Greg skirmished for more wood. Dr. Bentley, his coat off and shirt sleeves rolled up, constructed a "warm oven" with stones topped by a large baking tin. Then he built another.

Dick fried the trout, while Dr. Bentley started low fires under the two crude warming ovens. As fast as trout were fried they were dropped into one oven, Tom's bass being dropped into the other. Potatoes were boiling in one pot, tinned peas in another, and tinned string beans in still another. Tinned pudding was set in another pot of water to heat, while Mrs. Bentley made a sauce, and the girls set the table and made the other necessary preparations for the luncheon.

Presently the meal was ready, though the boys did not seat themselves until they had seen their welcome guests served.

"Daddy," murmured Laura, "I don't blame you for regretting your boyhood, if you had many trout feasts."

"How's the bass?" asked Tom, almost jealously.

"Just splendid," replied Laura, sampling her first fork full.

"You boys are camping in a fisherman's paradise," declared Dr. Bentley. "I don't blame you for liking this life. When I was a boy fresh water fish were almost as plentiful as salt water fish. Now, we rarely find any fresh water fish in the markets. I can't understand how this choice retreat for fishermen has escaped notice, unless it is because of the almost total lack of inhabitants in this section, and the miserable apologies for roads. Once again I must caution all of you young women not to be indiscreet and spoil this fisherman's paradise for your young friends by talking about it to anyone."

All four of the girls promised absolute secrecy.

After they had all satisfied their hunger, Dick asked Dr. Bentley all about the St. Clair Lake House. He learned that it was a fine, modern hotel, accommodating about one hundred and fifty guests. It was just on the edge of the good roads, Dr. Bentley explained; this side of the hotel no roads worthy of the name existed. Dick was very thoughtful after receiving the information, for he had something on his mind.

"How about that chauffeur of yours, doctor?" asked Dave suddenly.

"Oh, we left him with a comfortable luncheon," replied Dr. Bentley. "He can't leave the car, you know."

"Will you take him two or three trout, sir?" urged Dick.

"And a bass, sir?" added Reade.

"We'll wait for him to eat them in the car," replied the physician, "provided the poor fellow hasn't gorged himself on plainer food and has no room left for real fare like this."

When the time came that the guests must really leave, five of the boys accompanied the party to the road. Hazelton remained to watch the camp.

"Now, let's hustle!" urged Dick, as the car rolled out of sight. "When we get back to camp we have many long hours of work to do."

"Work of what kind?" inquired Tom.

"First of all," replied Prescott, with his most mysterious air, "we are going to build, close to camp, a make-believe ice-box. Then we're going to fill the box with ice."

"And what will all that be for?" Dave wanted to know.

"If you can't guess now," smiled young Prescott, his eyes gleaming, "you'll soon begin to see daylight through my plan! I don't know---but I believe that the plan I have in mind is going to work out in great shape!"

## CHAPTER XVII
## DICK MAKES FISH TALK

That's the longest eight miles I've ever done," muttered Hazelton.

"The map is wrong. It's a hundred and eight," affirmed Dave.

"No matter, if the trip turns out to have been wisely planned," remarked Dick, a wistful look coming into his eyes. "Of course, I may have overshot the mark."

"That's a chance we had to take," declared Dave promptly. "We won't be disappointed if we find that we haven't made such a big move, after all."

The three high school boys had halted in the shade of some trees by the highway. A quarter of a mile away, around the head of the body of water known as the third lake, stood a handsome hotel, the St. Clair Lake House.

It was now nearly nine o'clock in the morning. Dick and his two comrades had been on the way, over the rough road, propelling the heavily laden push cart, from which water now dripped from melting ice. The boys had built their ice-house, or ice-box, whichever one preferred to call it, and they had stocked it with ice from the cave. Dick, Dave and Greg had whipped up and down the stream in turn; Tom and Dan had trolled the lake for bass. As fast as the fish were brought in they were stored on the ice. After two days of hard fishing the boys arose before four o'clock in the morning, for Dick was now ready to test his venture.

"Stay close by that box, Harry," warned Dick, as he took hold of the handles of the push cart.

"Won't I, though?" Hazelton demanded.

Dick and Dave trudged onward, taking brief turns at the cart. Thus they entered the hotel grounds at the rear, continuing until they were close up to the rear porch. Then Dick ascended the steps and knocked at the door. As no one answered, he stepped into the corridor.

"What do you want here?" asked a well-dressed, portly man of fifty, who stepped out of a nearby room.

"I would like to see the manager, or steward, sir," Prescott replied.

"We don't want any help," replied the man.

"I haven't any help to offer, sir," Dick smiled. "Can I see the steward, or the manager?"

"I'm the proprietor, if that will do," answered the man, giving Dick a sharp look. He saw that his youthful visitor was evidently a well-bred boy, but that did not prove that Dick was not looking for work. College boys often serve as bell-boys or waiters at summer hotels.

"If you will step outside then, a moment, sir," Prescott continued, "I think I can show you the nicest lot of black bass you ever saw."

"A string of bass, eh?"

"No, sir; quite a load."

"I'll look at them," said the proprietor briefly.

When he saw the quantity of bass, and noted the plumpness of the fish, the proprietor was more interested. It is always a problem, with a summer hotel, to serve enough novel food. But the proprietor offered less than half the price Dick named. The high school boy, however, stuck to his price.

"I can't deal with you, then," said the owner, with a shake of the head, starting to reenter the hotel.

"The Kelway House is about a mile and a half below here, isn't it, sir?" asked Prescott, preparing to push the cart along.

"Yes; but they won't buy fish at that price."

"I'll try them, anyway, sir. Thank you for the trouble you've taken for me. Good morning, sir."

"Hold on, there," interrupted the hotel proprietor. "Perhaps I can offer you a little more."

In his own mind the hotel man was determined that the rival Kelway House should not have the chance to serve these bass.

More haggling followed, but Dick stuck to his price. In the end he got it. Scales were brought and the fish weighed. The total came to eighteen dollars and thirty-three cents.

"I suppose an even eighteen dollars will satisfy you?" asked the hotel man.

"Yes, sir," admitted the greatly delighted Prescott.

While the money was being counted over, Dave slipped away with the push cart.

"In about ten minutes, sir," said Dick, after he had pocketed the money and had thanked the hotel man, "I'll have something else to show you."

"What?" asked the man, eyeing Dick keenly.

"Now, if you don't mind, sir," coaxed Dick, with a smile, "I'd rather not destroy, in advance, the keen delight you're going to feel when you see the next cartload."

"How many of these cartloads have you lying around?" asked the proprietor quickly.

"The next one will be also the last, sir. May I call you out when my friends get here with it?"

"I---I guess so," assented the hotel man, and then went inside. Dick found a seat on a nearby bench and waited.

Dave and Harry presently came along with the cart. Dick once more went after his prospective purchaser.

"What have you now---more bass?" asked the hotel man, eyeing the heavy box on the cart. Water was dripping from the ice and running to the ground.

"No, sir; just look!" begged Prescott, lifting some jute bagging from the top of the box, then digging down through the top layer of cracked ice.

"Brook trout?" cried the hotel man. "Where on earth did you get them?"

"We have a factory where we turn 'em out nights, sir," volunteered Dave, with a grin.

"What do you want for them---same price as for the bass?" demanded the proprietor.

"We could hardly afford to do that, you know," Prescott replied. "Down in a town like Gridley these brook trout ought to retail for a dollar and a half a pound. We'll offer them to you, sir, at sixty cents a pound---flat."

"Take 'em away!" ordered the hotel man, with an air of finality. This time it was plain that he did not propose to purchase.

"You won't be sorry after we're gone, will you?" asked Dick politely.

"I can't afford to put sixty-cents-a-pound fish on my bill of fare," said the hotel man.

At this moment two well-dressed, prosperous-looking, middle-aged men came strolling around the corner of the building. As Dick was about to cover his fish one of them caught sight of the speckled beauties, and stopped short.

"Hello! Aren't these fine, Johnson?" the man demanded of the proprietor. "Going to buy these trout for the hotel?"

"I can't afford to put such costly fish on the bill of fare," replied Johnson candidly.

"Man, you don't have to," replied the other. "Send these trout to the grill-room ice-box. Let guests who want brook trout order them as extras. Why, I'll eat a few of these myself, if you serve 'em."

"Certainly," nodded the other man.

Proprietor Johnson had caught a new idea from the suggestion of serving the trout as an "extra" in the grill-room of the hotel. All of a sudden he began to scent a profit.

"All right, young man," smiled Mr. Johnson. "Begin to unload. I'll have the scales brought out again."

The weight proved to be a little over one hundred pounds. Dick accepted an even sixty dollars, while Harry Hazelton nearly strangled himself in his efforts to keep from cheering lustily.

This money, too, was counted out.

"Are you going to bring any more fish this way?" asked Mr. Johnson.

"I can hardly say as to that, sir," Dick hesitated.

"If you do, I can't agree positively to buy, but I'll be glad, anyway, if you'll give me the first chance. I will see how these trout 'go' in the grill-room in the meantime."

"We'll give you the first call, sir," Dick nodded. "Thank you very much for this morning's business."

"That boy is a budding merchant," thought Johnson, staring after Dick as the three high school boys trundled their cart away. But in this estimate the hotel man chanced to be wrong.

"Let's hurry up and get away from the hotel---a long way off," urged Hazelton.

"Why?" asked Dave. "It was a fine place---for us."

"Yes; but I want to yell, with all my might," Darry declared. "Seventy-eight dollars---think of it!"

"Nothing to get excited about," Dick declared calmly.

"When did we ever make so much money in life same time before?" blurted Hazelton.

"Never, perhaps," Prescott admitted. "We made money, this time, because we had something that everyone wants, and the supply of which isn't large. We would have made far more money if we had had a cart full of diamonds in the rough."

"What are you talking about?" demanded Hazelton. "We don't know where to find diamonds."

"I didn't say that we did," Dick rejoined. "But we had something that is rare, and in demand. The rarer a thing is that everyone wants the better price can be had for it. The bass didn't bring anywhere near as much money as the trout, just because people don't call for black bass as much as they will for brook trout."

They were entering the little village beyond the hotel. They had to go there in order to mail their letters, for all the boys had taken advantage of this opportunity to write home.

"We'll be nervous with this seventy-eight dollars in camp, in addition to the few other dollars we have," Dave suggested.

"We won't keep a lot of money in camp," Dick replied. "I'm going to buy a money order for seventy-five dollars, payable to myself, and send it to my father to hold for me until we get back. Then I'll cash the order in Gridley and turn the money into our common fund."

"And we'll add to that fund," proposed Hazelton eagerly.

"If the bass and the trout hold out," supplemented Dick.

"Say, wouldn't it be mighty nice if only we could get some home letters here?" asked Hazelton, as the three left the cart at the curb and turned to enter the post-office.

"We can look for home letters on our next trip here," Dick suggested. "On Tom's, Greg's and Dan's letters I'm going to add a note on the outside of the envelope to the effect that letters may be sent to this office for us. And I'm going to add a postscript to my letter to my father and mother. You fellows had better do the same thing."

Dick's first move was to get a money order blank and fill out his application. Then all hands attended to their postscripts.

This done they went outside.

"There's a little grove down that street," said Dave, pointing. "Why not go down there and take a brief nap?"

"I want a long one," Dick laughed. "Traveling over that road was harder work than I've ever done on the football field."

Their nap lasted until a little after noon.

"Whee! But I'm hungry," grumbled Hazelton.

"I think we may feel justified in finding a restaurant, and getting a good meal," assented Dick.

"I want a steak for mine," proposed Darry. "It seems a year since we've had one."

"Great idea!" nodded Dick. "And, while we're about it, we'll get steaks and some stewing meat the last thing before we leave town and take it back to the fellows. We've had so much fish that red meat will hit a tender spot with all the fellows."

"It will make a big hit with Tom Reade, I know," laughed Hazelton.

Pushing the cart through the street, the high school boys found a restaurant that looked as though it would be within reach of their purses. The boys put their cart in a back yard, then went in and asked permission to wash up. This being granted, they soon after took seats at a table in the restaurant.

It was an odd little place, equipped with several booths, each containing a table and seats for four persons.

"We'll take the booth away down at the end of the room, where we won't be seen by better-dressed people," proposed Dave.

Accordingly they occupied the last booth in the row. There they ordered a meal that made their mouths water in advance.

Hazelton, poking his head out of the booth as he heard some one enter, hastily drew it in again.

"Guess who's coming!" he whispered.

"Can't," replied Dick.

"Dodge and Bayliss," replied Harry.

"Keep out of sight, and don't talk," ordered Prescott.

Bert Dodge and his chum came down the room, taking the booth next to that of the high school boys, yet without seeing Dick and his chums.

When the waiter appeared Dodge ordered two ice creams.

"Queer what became of the mucker gang," observed Bayliss, after the waiter had departed.

"Not a bit queer," retorted Bert. "That was why I wanted to meet you here this morning. I've found out where they are."

"How did you find out?" demanded Bayliss.

"Do you see this post card?" demanded Bert, laying a card on the table. "It was written by Laura Bentley to Susie Sharp, and mentions their having had lunch at the camp of the high school muckers. And this message gives a clear enough idea of where their camp is, too. Laura must have dropped the card in the street, for that's where I found it."

"Say, that's a great find!" chuckled Bayliss.

"You may wager that it is," grinned Dodge. "We broke up one night of sleep for the muckers with those bombs, but I've an idea that the night we shot off sixty rounds of blank shotgun shells that they had already moved. But now I have a brand-new one that we can use and make them break camp and run for home as fast as they can go. Then we'll pass the story of their scare all around Gridley, and they'll never hear the last of the laugh against them."

"I'm all attention, old fellow!" Bayliss protested eagerly.

"So are we!" thought Dick grimly, as he glanced at Dave and Harry.

## CHAPTER XVIII
## A KETTLE OF HOT WATER FOR SOMEONE

It was a wonderfully elaborate scheme to which the high school boys were privileged to listen. Such a scheme, really showed Dodge, in a way, to be possessed of more brains than people in Gridley commonly credited him with possessing.

But Dick smiled at Dave Darrin's scowl as the plot was unfolded in the next booth.

Fortunately for Dick and his chums the steak order was delayed in the serving. Thus Dodge and Bayliss finished their ice cream and left the place without discovering the presence of their intended victims.

"Say, aren't that pair just going to enjoy themselves at our expense?" chuckled Hazelton, after the plotters had left.

"Unless I miss my guess, they're going to dance to our music to-night," laughed Dick gleefully.

Their meal was served soon after, and eaten with relish. As soon as it had been finished Dick asked the waiter for a sheet of paper and envelope.

"Don't worry about any weird doings you may hear of from our camp," Prescott wrote his mother. "We've just learned of a big scare Dodge and Bayliss are planning to spring on us up at our camp. We're going to turn the tables on them---that's all. But I write this for fear you may hear some awful tales when that pair reach Gridley."

As they left the restaurant, Dick returned to the post-office, mailing this second letter to his mother.

"Now, we must buy a few things here," Dick explained to his friends. "Then we must get out of this village by a back road, and we must make sure that we don't run into that pair of ex-soreheads."

The "sorehead" reference, as readers of our "*High School Boys Series*" will recall, had to do with Dodge and Bayliss, ere they had been chased out of Gridley High School. These boys had belonged to the notorious "sorehead faction" in the high school football squad.

Going in different directions, Dick, Dave and Harry were able to make all their needed purchases in a short time. Right after that, they got out of the village, and back upon the rough trail for camp without having met their enemies.

It was nearly seven o'clock when the three travelers, all but fagged out, pushed their cart in sight of camp and gave a hail that brought the other chums running to meet them.

First of all, word was passed as to the successful outcome of the fish-selling expedition.

"I thought you fellows would bring us some fresh meat," Tom cried, when Dave unloaded the cart. "Fresh vegetables, too? Wow! Won't we live? I told the fellows not to try to get supper until you got back, as you'd be sure to bring something that would make us sorry we had eaten. We've the fires all ready."

"And now, listen!" commanded Dick Prescott, after the first preparations had been made for supper.

Thereupon the young leader of Dick & Co. repeated the plot they had heard Dodge and Bayliss unfold that noon.

"Hang those two heathens!" sputtered Tom Reade indignantly.

"Oh, I'm glad they're coming," laughed Dick. "All I hope is that nothing will happen to keep them from coming to-night."

Then Dick outlined his plan. Tom Read, after listening for a few moments, lay on the ground, rolling over and over in his glee.

"Wow! But won't that be great?" demanded Greg, laughing until the tears ran from his eyes.

"Say, we mustn't talk any more now. We must eat supper, and then get ready if we're to play the reception committee successfully tonight."

At a very early hour, considering the lateness of the evening meal, Reade, with his knack in woodwork, and with no other tool than his jackknife, had fashioned the stocks for two "rifles." These Hazelton carefully treated with mud from the lake so as to give them a dark color.

"If the guns are seen by the light of the campfire, the stocks and barrels ought to be of different colors," Dick explained.

Dave was now fashioning two straight sticks into semblance of rifle barrels. These were lightly treated with mud and fastened to the two stocks. Then two additional "rifles" were to be manufactured.

Other work was performed, and all was gotten in readiness. Prescott had a number of mysterious-looking little packages that he had bought in the village.

"Oh, dear, but I hope nothing happens to keep Dodge and Bayliss from coming to-night," breathed Tom, as he labored fast. "David, little giant, hurry up with those barrels. There can be no telling how soon we shall have to defend ourselves with these 'Quaker' guns!"

As they worked, the high school boys indulged in many a chuckle.

"It takes something like this to keep me awake to-night," Dick yawned. "If there were no excitement coming, I'm so dead sleepy that I could go right into dreamland standing up."

"So could I," chirped Dave. "But I manage to keep awake by enjoying the thought of how thoroughly we'll wake up someone else tonight!"

"If our plans don't miscarry," warned Dick.

"Please don't croak about failure or disappointment," begged Tom tragically. "My warm, impulsive young heart won't stand any disappointment to-night."

So they toiled on, their preparations all along the line taking shape rapidly.

By ten o'clock they had everything completed, including the manufacture of the "Quaker" rifles.

"Now, to our posts," chuckled Dick, after a rapid distribution of things from the packages brought up from the village.

The campfire was allowed to burn low. Some light was still needed for the full success of their plans.

Tom and Dan took up their stand in front of the tent, each armed with a "Quaker" gun.

## CHAPTER XIX
## BERT DODGE HEARS FRIGHTFUL NEWS

Half an hour passed. At last there came the long-drawn, doleful note of the screech owl.

It was but an amateurish imitation; an Indian would have treated it with contempt, but it was well enough done to deceive untrained ears.

Tom glanced at Danny Grin, smiling quietly. The imitation note of the screech owl was a signal from Dick that Dodge and Bayliss had arrived, and were starting their nonsense.

Still Tom did not speak of this to Dan. There could be no telling whether Dodge or Bayliss might be within hearing already. So Tom and Dan, gripping their quite harmless weapons, became more alert in appearance.

It was true enough that Dodge and Bayliss were now on the scene. They had hidden their car off at the side of the road, a mile or more below, and had crept forward with their outfit for the night's big scare.

Dodge carried half a dozen large hot-air balloons, which he had made for the purpose. Under the other arm be carried a package that looked as though it had come from a department store.

Bayliss, a broad grin on his face, carried the working parts of a new style siren whistle, intended for automobiles, but a machinist had succeeded in flutting some new notes and effects into the screech of this ear-splitter.

"I hope they won't take the noise of this siren for the cry of a screech owl," whispered Bayliss, as the pair stole stealthily along.

"If they do, they'll soon get over that idea, and find their real fright up in the air," Bert Dodge whispered in response.

"I wonder how much further on their camp is, or whether we're anywhere near it?" Bayliss asked.

"We'll soon know how close we are, for the lake can't be much further on. I just caught sight of the water in the starlight," Bert answered.

How astounded both mischief makers would have been had they known that certain members of Dick & Co. were even now trailing them.

"There's the tent!" whispered Dodge suddenly, checking his Companion, as they came to a spot on the slope where they could see the white of the canvas faintly displayed by the glow from a dying campfire.

"Two of them are about, too!" muttered Bayliss disgustedly.

"Then they're all the more certain to see what they're going to see soon," chuckled his companion. "Only we must work quickly."

Bayliss separated one of the balloons from the string held by Bert. The package was opened and from it Bayliss took and fitted over the balloon enough filmy gauze to cover it to a length of six or seven feet. Tying a longer string to the balloon, Bayliss allowed the white, filmy mass to soar upward. When the balloon had reached a height of twenty feet above the near-by tree tops, Bayliss made it fast to a tree trunk. Then he and Dodge skipped hastily to a point some eighty yards away, where they speedily sent up another. In a very short time all six balloons were flying on the night air, each with its trail of white fleecy stuff hanging therefrom.

"They do look like ghosts flying in the air, don't they?" demanded Bayliss exultantly.

"Not to me," muttered Bert. "But that's because I know what they're made of."

"Let's hustle now with the rest," urged Bayliss.

"Right you are," agreed Bert.

They hurried along, going a bit nearer to the camp, until Dodge pointed to a tangle of bushes.

"That'll be a good place to hide with the siren. You get in there with it, but don't start it until about sixty seconds after you hear the big noise. Then I'll hustle right back here to you."

"Don't let any of Dick Prescott's friends catch you," urged Bayliss, who would have gasped had he known that at that moment two of them crouched close enough to hear every word.

Now Bert hastened down the slope, carrying a fireworks' bomb very much like those that he and Bayliss had set off on the opposite side of the lake on another evening long to be remembered.

Treading cautiously, Bert reached a point not far distant from the doorway of the camp tent. Here, crouching in the screening bushes, Bert placed the bomb in position. It was only a fireworks' bomb of the kind used on Fourth of July nights. It was harmless enough to one who stood more than thirty feet from it.

"The fuse will burn a minute before it goes off," murmured Bert to himself. "That will give me almost time to reach Bayliss before the big noise comes. The noise will bring them all out of the tent. Then the remainder of our programme will do the rest."

But, even as Bert reached for the match with which to touch off the fuse he heard Dalzell call in a voice audible at the distance:

"Look at those things up in the air, Tom!"

"He has sighted our 'ghosts,'" laughed Bert to himself.

"They must be some sort of signal kites, flown by the moonshiners," answered Reade in an interested tone.

"Kites! Is that what he takes our ghosts for?" wondered Bert Dodge in deep disgust.

But the mention of the word "moonshiners" gave the listener a start. In a general way he knew that "moonshiner" is the term applied to men who try to cheat the United States Revenue Service by distilling liquors on which they pay no tax. Bert had heard that moonshiners are deadly men, indeed, and that they make little of shooting down the government officers who are sent to ferret out their hiding places and arrest them.

"I wish we hadn't run into those moonshiners," said Danny, rather dolefully. "And I wish Dick hadn't thought it necessary to go and send word to the United States authorities. I'm afraid there's going to be an awful row here to-night."

"What's that?" wondered Bert, pricking up his ears.

"I rather wish Dick hadn't been in such an awful rush," Tom admitted slowly. "Anyway, we fellows should have gotten out of here and left it to the marshals to have it all their own way. I'm afraid there is going to be a big fight to-night, and these old woods may be full of humming bullets. And I'm worried about Dick, too, going off as guide to the marshals. There were only eight of the marshals, and, even with four of our fellows, they still have to face nearly twenty of the moonshiners---and I'll wager that the moonshiners are all desperate fighters."

"Oh, dear!" wailed Danny Grin.

Bert Dodge's face was a study. With the prospect of a running fight between United States' marshals and desperate moonshiners about to take place, these woods seemed likely to be anything but a safe place.

"At least, the marshals did a decent thing in leaving us rifles here to protect ourselves with," Dan Dalzell continued.

Raising his head, Bert took a long look at the camp. Not far away stood Tom Reade, the outlines of a rifle in his grasp showing very distinctly. Dalzell was over nearer the shadow of the tent, yet Bert made sure that Dalzell had a rifle also.

"Gracious! There is likely to be real enough trouble in the woods to-night!" muttered Bert. "Those boys didn't have guns when they left Gridley. The authorities have probably furnished them."

Just then a popping fire rang out further up the lake slope.

"There it goes!" almost yelled Danny Grin. "The marshals have run into the moonshiners. The fight is on. Oh, I hope none of our fellows are being hit!"

Certainly the firing continued briskly. Dodge forgot all about lighting the fuse of the fireworks' bomb.

Instead, he crouched low, then darted from the bushes, running as fast as he could to the point where he had left his companion.

"In here!" chuckled Bayliss gleefully. "I didn't know you had anything with you but the bomb, Bert."

"That's all I did have," whispered Dodge, white-faced. "Hustle out of here, Bayliss!"

"What's the matter?"

"Hear that firing?"

"I thought you had been setting off fire crackers, Bert."

"Fire crackers nothing!" ejaculated Bert, his face ghastly. "Man alive, that's a fight going on up the slope between United States officers and a lot of desperate moonshiners! There goes the firing again."

Bayliss heard it; he couldn't help that.

Then still nearer rang out the firing.

"We've got to get out of here as fast as our legs will take us," Bert insisted. "Hustle before the bullets reach us."

At that moment Dave Darrin broke from cover, running as fast as his legs could carry him. As he raced toward camp Darrin called:

"Reade! Danny! This is Darrin. Get ready to run or fight. It's a fearful affair. Four of the marshals were down when I left, and Dick Prescott is done for, too! Oh, it's fearful! There won't be any of the government party left!"

Apparent terror rang in Darrin's voice as he ran forward flourishing his "Quaker" rifle.

"Great Scott!" groaned Bayliss, trying to rise and run, though his legs shook under him.

"Buck up! Don't be a coward!" hissed Dodge, seizing his companion by the arm. "Come on! Run for it---before we're hit."

Thus the two made their escape, running, stumbling through the woods, heading blindly for the spot where they had left their car.

Back of them fresh sounds of firing rang out. How could the frightened, dazed fugitives know that it was Dick Prescott, pursuing, and dropping lighted strings of fire crackers as he ran?

"It's a running fight, and coming right our way!" gasped Bert.

"Let's drop down and crawl to safety!" almost screamed Bayliss.

"No, you don't!" retorted Dodge angrily. "Our only safety lies in getting into that car and throwing the engine wide open. I don't care if we wreck the car if only we can cover a couple of miles of ground first. Run! Hustle!"

Had he suffered from a little keener fear, Bayliss would have collapsed utterly. As it was, fear lent him extra speed. He fairly tore over the ground, darting through bushes, plunging on in headlong haste. Bert kept with him.

"We'll soon be all right," cried Dodge encouragingly. "Now, jump right across the road. Our car is in there, and headed the right way."

Just as they reached the car and Bert's pale face showed right in front of the headlights a third figure dashed up.

Harry Hazelton, his head swathed in a red-stained bandage, and what appeared to be blood dripping from his left arm, sprang at them, the butt of his rifle showing, but its barrel wrapped in his jacket.

---

## CHAPTER XX
## A FRENZIED RIDE TO SAFETY

"Wait!" gasped Hazelton. "You've got to take me, too."

"Not much," hissed Bayliss, his voice trembling. "This car is built only for two."

"You've got to take me, I tell you," Harry insisted, his voice trembling. "Do you think I'm going to be left behind?"

"This car is built for-----" Bayliss started to insist again.

"Then you will stay behind, Bayliss, at that rate," Harry retorted. "Remember, I am able to enforce my wishes. Do I go, too?"

Bert had started the engine, and now sprang in at the wheel. Hazelton leaped in also, taking the other seat.

Bayliss, quivering in every muscle, leaped in, crouching between them.

"I see that you've decided to come along with us," mocked Harry.

"Hang you!" snarled Bayliss. "If you didn't have that gun we'd see about it."

"Start her, fast, Dodge!" ordered Harry.

With a roar of the engine the car lurched forward.

"What happened to the others in your crowd?" asked Bert in a weak voice, as he steered carefully down the rough road.

"All flat---all five of 'em!" affirmed Harry, but be neglected to state that his five chums were lying on the ground, rolling over in their mirth.

"None of 'em got away, then, but you?" chattered Bayliss.

"Do you think I'd let you take this car away from here?" demanded Hazelton indignantly, "if there were any more of our fellows to get away from here? What would you fellows count for if it were necessary to save more of my friends?"

"It must have been a fearful fight," shivered Dodge.

"It was," said Harry grimly, striving with all his might to keep from bursting out in laughter. "I never had any idea that a gun fight was such an awful thing!"

"Prescott got his, then?" asked Bayliss.

"All five of my friends," replied Hazelton, in a choking voice. "And I've some traces of the fight to show myself."

"How badly bit are you?" demanded Dodge.

"I'll last all right until I get to Gridley," Harry predicted, "if you fellows don't keep me talking too much."

"I didn't intend going to Gridley to-night," Dodge replied.

"Yes, you will," Hazelton replied firmly. "I must go to Gridley. You drive straight there. I'll hold you responsible, if you don't."

Bert began to believe that he **would** be held accountable if he failed to take Hazelton to Gridley, so he gave in without protest. At any rate, both Dodge and Bayliss wanted to get as far as possible from the recent "horror," and as speedily as they could do it.

"There's no chance of our being attacked on the road to Gridley?" asked Bayliss by and by, in a quavering voice.

"No," replied Hazelton. "The lake will be between us and the trouble makers."

It was rough going most of the way. Hazelton was disinclined to talk. Bayliss' nerves were too shattered for him to feel like indulging in conversation. Dodge, white-faced, his cap pulled well down over his eyes, showed all that he knew about running a car carefully and as speedily as was possible over such rough roads.

It was after two o'clock in the morning when the car turned into the stretch of Main Street, Gridley.

"We'll go to the police station with the fearful news," proposed Bert Dodge.

"No, we won't," retorted Hazelton. "We'll go to the 'Blade' office. Mr. Pollock, the editor, is one of Dick's best friends, and he'll know better than anyone else in town what ought to be done."

So with hands that trembled Bert drove the car up in front of the "Morning Blade" office. All three leaped out, Dodge and Bayliss eager to get into the glow of lights and among human beings.

As Harry's feet struck the sidewalk he remembered his character as a wounded man and tried to totter up the steps in a realistic fashion.

In the "Blade" building the press was rumbling busily as the inside pages of the paper were being run off.

Mr. Pollock, all alone in the editorial part of the plant, looked up in astonishment as the ghastly-hued Dodge and Bayliss appeared. The editor's feeling turned to consternation when he saw Hazelton's seemingly pitiable condition.

"Hazelton, what can have happened?" gasped the editor, leaping to his feet.

"Take me into another room!" pleaded Harry.  "You two fellows," indicating Bert and his chum, "stay out here."

Though he didn't guess the answer, Mr. Pollock led young Hazelton into the mailing room and turned on the light there.

"Sh-h-h!" warned Hazelton, his face lighting up impishly.  "Dodge and Bayliss tried to play a trick on Dick & Co. and Prescott has turned the laugh on them."

"But these blood-stained bandages?" questioned the astounded editor.

"It's stuff that is used for coloring strawberry ice cream.  Dick bought it at a store.  Looks like the real thing, doesn't it?"

"It looked real enough to give me a bad turn," admitted the editor dryly.

Then, in whispers, Harry told the story as rapidly as he could. Mr. Pollock's face took on a broader grin as he listened.

"I'd hate to have young Prescott for my enemy," confessed the "Blade's" editor. "But this is the most atrocious joke I've ever known him to put up."

"We had to put a stop to Dodge and Bayliss," Harry smiled.  "Perhaps you'd better go back to Dodge and Bayliss, now---but please don't let 'em know that it's all a joke."

"I won't spoil the thing," promised the editor, and hastened out.

"I'll be with you in just a minute, gentlemen," nodded Mr. Pollock to Dodge and Bayliss, as he entered the editorial room, then sprang into the telephone closet, closing the door after him.

Mr. Pollock telephoned the sheriff of the county, and also the officer in charge at the Gridley police station, giving the officials a hint of the joke at the second lake, so they wouldn't rush away on a fool's errand in case the wild story reached their ears.

"Now I'll listen to what you two may have to tell me," announced Mr. Pollock, coming out of the telephone closet.  "Then I'll have to ask you to hurry away, as Hazelton will have to be attended to and many things done. Talk fast, if you please."

Dodge and Bayliss poured out what they knew of the night's business.

"And how did you two happen to be there?" inquired Mr. Pollock.

"Oh, we---we---we were touring in that part of the country, and were fixing a break-down when Hazelton came running up," stammered Bert Dodge.

"It was fortunate, indeed, for Hazelton, that you had that break-down," replied the editor. Then his manner showed Dodge and Bayliss that it was time for them to go. Both were glad to get out of the "Blade" office, for they feared to stand too much questioning from one as keen as the newspaper man.

## CHAPTER XXI
## REAL NEWS AND "PUNK HEROES"

Bayliss, no matter what happens," whispered Dodge, as the two young men climbed into the car outside, "don't you ever let it be found out that we went to the camp of Dick & Co. to play a joke on Prescott and the others. The awful way this night's work has turned out would make the town too hot for us."

"Don't you be afraid of my becoming loose-tongued," chattered Bayliss. "Ugh! I don't believe I'll ever want to talk to anyone again. Bert, do you really believe that all of the fellows but Hazelton were really wiped out?"

"They---they must have been," gasped Dodge.

"It's fearful!"

"It is," Dodge assented, as he threw on the speed. "I never liked Prescott, but to-night's awful work is something that I'd have been willing to have saved him from if there had been a way to do it.

"Which way are you heading?" asked Bayliss suddenly.

"To Dr. Bentley's. If he's at home, I want to hustle him to the 'Blade' office. I believe he's the Hazelton family's physician. Bayliss, any sign of attention to Hazelton on our part will look well for us at a time when we're likely to be asked many questions about how we came to be so near to their camp. We've got to be mighty careful, or in the excitement that will follow the awful fate of Prescott and his friends the town might grow so hot for us that we'd be all but lynched. Now, no one can prove that we weren't on a trip, and that our car broke down on the road; that we heard the fire of rifles, and the next thing we knew Hazelton, badly wounded, came rushing up to us, and that we brought him in as fast as we could. Now, let's make up a story as to just what trip we were taking when we broke down on the road a mile from their camp."

The two plotters quickly planned out their story.

"Here's Dr. Bentley's office," said Dodge, as they turned a corner. "You stay in the car, Bayliss. I can attend to this better." So Dodge was soon pouring a tale of woe and tragedy up through the night speaking tube into the astounded, half-suspicious ears of Dr. Bentley.

Then Bert Dodge drove with Bayliss to the latter's home, after which Bert quakingly drove the car around to his own home, where he roused his father to hear the strange news. Nor was it long ere the whole Dodge family was listening, awe struck.

In the meantime Hazelton was exhibiting to Mr. Pollock, with many a chuckle, the "Quaker" rifle that he had brought into the office wrapped in his jacket. Harry also displayed the bottle of strawberry coloring for ice cream that had supplied the color to his head bandage.

Ting-a-ling! rang the telephone. It was Dr. Bentley on the wire, inquiring whether Dodge had been guilty of a hoax in calling him up to go to the "Blade" office in order to attend Hazelton.

With many a chuckle Mr. Pollock told Dr. Bentley, under injunction of secrecy, the story of the night's doings. When Dr. Bentley heard the story of this latest "outrage" by Dick & Co. he laughed heartily. "Well, well," he mused, "what will Dick and his friends be up to next?"

"Hazelton," ordered Mr. Pollock, "you take the old overcoats you'll find in that closet and arrange them on top of one of these long tables. Get some sleep. I'll call you in time for you to get word to the parents of Dick & Co. after six in the morning. As for me, I shall expect to get no sleep until I've put this big news story in shape."

Yet that morning's issue of the "Blade" didn't contain a word on the subject. Mr. Pollock was wise enough to write the story, then save it for appearance at the proper time.

By six o'clock Harry was aroused. A closed cab, its driver pledged to secrecy, was at the door to carry Harry on his rounds. He visited the parents of all the members of Dick & Co., informing them that the story they might soon hear was not based on any facts that need alarm them.

Before seven o'clock that morning Dodge and Bayliss, wild-eyed and haggard looking, met at Bert's home. Mr. Dodge took them, soon after, down onto Main Street with him.

The first public whisper of the news sent it flying fast over Gridley.

By nine o'clock Main Street was unwontedly crowded. Groups of men, women and young people everywhere discussed the "awful news." Those who had been privileged to hear Dodge and Bayliss tell the story were looked upon as most interesting people.

Of course a few Gridleyites tried to find the parents of the "slain" boys and express their sympathy, but the parents of the members of Dick & Co., strangely enough, could not be found.

With many repetitions of the story, Dodge and Bayliss almost unintentionally began to picture themselves as heroes, who had risked their lives in order to bring the single survivor away to safety.

"There's some good in young Dodge and Bayliss, after all," was a not infrequent comment that morning.

"It must have taken real nerve, anyway, for them to make that thrilling rescue of Hazelton," said others.

So Dodge and Bayliss, much to their astonishment and not a little to their delight, found themselves somewhat in the hero class. Their exhausted, wild-eyed, haggard appearance gave more color to the story of the harrowing experience they claimed to have undergone in rescuing Hazelton from that awful field of carnage up by the second lake.

At ten o'clock Mr. Pollock's automobile drew up at the rear door of the "Blade" building. Hazelton slipped out, crouching low in the car, that he might not be seen and recognized, while Mr. Pollock and his star reporter, Len Spencer, openly entered and drove away. They made straight for the wilderness camp of Dick & Co. Once out of the town Harry rose to a comfortable seat, and made up some of his lost sleep during the trip.

One thing that puzzled the excited citizens of Gridley was the placid way in which the chief of police and the sheriff of the county appeared to take the sad news.

Mr. Pollock drove his car as close to camp as he could, after which he and his companions hurried over the uneven ground until they came upon five high school boys seated outside.

"How did it all work out, Harry?" shouted Dick, leaping up as soon as he saw his approaching comrade.

"It is working in great shape, you young scoundrel!" roared Editor Pollock, gripping Dick Prescott's hand. "And the yarn is going to make the biggest and best midsummer sensation that the 'Blade' has ever had!"

Mr. Pollock and Len Spencer remained at camp for something like an hour and a half, enjoying a trout luncheon before they left.

It was four o'clock in the afternoon when editor and reporter reached the "Blade" office.

At five o'clock the "Blade" put out a bulletin, around which a crowd collected in no time. The crowd grew to such proportions that the policeman on the beat tried in vain to make it "move on."

That bulletin read:

"Lake Tragedy All a Tremendous Hoax: Read the 'Blade's' six o'clock extra."

At a few minutes before six o'clock Len Spencer began to arrange one of the street windows of the "Blade" office.

First of all, from hooks, he suspended Dodge and Bayliss' "ghosts" of the night before.

"What does that mean?" asked the wondering onlookers.

Then an unexploded bomb bearing the trademark of the Sploderite Company was put in the window. It was followed by the *siren* whistle that Bayliss had dropped in his flight. Then four "Quaker" wooden guns, a red-stained bandage and a partly used bottle of strawberry ice cream coloring appeared.

Promptly at six o'clock newsboys appeared on the street with the exciting announcement:

"Extree! Extree 'Bla-ade'! All about Dick & Co.'s latest! The best joke of the season!"

Papers went off like hot cakes. Before the evening was over more than two thousand copies of that edition had been sold. Many more than two thousand people had crowded to the "Blade's" show window to catch a glimpse of the exhibits described in the rollicking news story.

"Pshaw! Dodge and Bayliss, the heroes!" shouted one man in the crowd, as he ran his eye through the story.

"Punk heroes!" answered someone else in the crowd.

The story was cleverly told. Dodge and Bayliss were not mentioned by name, but described only as a pair of amateur jokers whose plans had miscarried. Yet the plain, unvarnished story cast complete ridicule over Bert and his friend.

While the fever of the reading crowd was at its height someone shouted:

"Here they come now!"

Bert and Bayliss had just driven around the corner in the car. During the last three hours both had slept at Bert's, but now they were out and abroad again in order to hear the latest developments.

Suddenly a hush fell over the crowd. Bert and Bayliss were allowed to drive in silence to the curb.

Then, just as suddenly, a dozen men leaped at the car, dragging both youths to the sidewalk.

"Wha-a-at's wrong?" faltered Bert Dodge.

"We'll soon show you!" came the jeering answer of the captors.

Then a mighty shout of derision went up from the crowd.

## CHAPTER XXII
## TOM TELLS THE BIG SECRET

Take 'em to the horse trough!" roared more than one voice.

So Dodge and Bayliss, the centre---of a jeering, resolute crowd, were dragged down the street a short distance. The crowd swelled in numbers.

"Stand Dodge on the edge of the trough, and make him read the paper!" shouted one man.

That was accordingly done. Bert was shaking so that he had to be supported in the place chosen for him.

Bayliss was whimpering in abject terror.

"Now, read this in the 'Blade,' Dodge," ordered a tormentor, shoving a paper forward. "Read it aloud."

Bert began, in a wavering voice.

"Louder!" yelled a score of voices from different points in the crowd.

Bert tried to obey, but his voice was shaky.

However, he read the article through to the end, while the crowd waited ominously.

"Heroes, weren't you?" jeered many voices when white-faced Bert had finished the reading.

"Duck him!" came the answer.

Bert was well splashed in the water of the trough. Then Bayliss shared the same fate.

"Now---git! Travel fast---both of you!" came the order.

Nor did Bert or Bayliss need any further commands. Frightened as they were, they nevertheless summoned the strength to run desperately. No one struck them, even in fun. Only jeers assailed them. Neither boy made any effort to get back to the automobile, but both kept on until they had turned a corner and vanished from sight.

"Pity we didn't have some rifle fire to tie to their coat tails," laughed one citizen. For the "Blade" had made it plain that firecrackers, exploded in packs, had provided the sounds of gun fire up at the camp on the second lake.

"Oh, we'll make somebody sweat for this outrage!" quivered Bert, his face dark and scowling, as he and Bayliss slowed up on a quiet side street. "There are laws in this land! We might even get damages out of someone!"

"I feel as if I had collected about all the damage I want for a few days," muttered Bayliss, gazing down ruefully at his drenched clothing and water-logged shoes.

"I wonder who'll take this car home?" asked one of the men in front of the "Blade" office.

"Where is my son?" inquired Mr. Dodge, pushing his way through the crowd without any suspicion of what had lately happened. "Isn't my son here to take this car home?"

"I doubt if he'll come back," replied one man, with a twinkle in his eyes.

"'Blade'? Extree 'Blade'?" demanded a newsboy, holding out a paper.

"Better take one, Mr. Dodge," advised a man in the crowd. "Mighty interesting reading in this extra!"

Almost mechanically the banker paid for a paper, folded it, then stepped into the automobile.

On his arrival home, and after having turned the car over to his chauffeur, Mr. Dodge went to his library, despite the fact that he knew his dinner was waiting.

There he spread out the extra "Blade" on a table and began to read the featured news story.

As he read the elder Dodge flushed deeply. Though the names of Bert and Bayliss were not mentioned, he had no difficulty in connecting them with the ludicrous story.

Turning, Mr. Dodge rang. A man servant answered.

"Mrs. Dodge wishes to know, sir, when you are coming to dinner," said the man.

"Ask Mrs. Dodge, from me kindly to let the dinner go on, and say that I am busy, now, but will come to the table as soon as I am at leisure. Then ask Mr. Bert to come here to me at once."

Bert entered. He had removed his wet garments, and put on fresh clothing. He had been at dinner when interrupted by his father's message.

"This extraordinary story in the 'Blade' refers to you, does it not?" inquired the banker, shoving the paper before the young man.

"Yes, sir," Bert admitted sulkily.

"You and your friend, Bayliss, have been making fools of yourselves, have you?"

"No, sir," cried Bert. "We were made fools of by others."

"When it comes to making a fool of yourself, Bert, no one else is swift enough to get ahead of you," replied his father witheringly. "So, you have succeeded in making the entire family objects of ridicule once more? I had hoped that that sort of thing had ceased when I sent you away to a private school."

"We were imposed on," flushed Bert angrily. "Nor has the outrage stopped there. Bayliss and I were seized in front of the 'Blade' office, and taken over to the horse trough and ducked!"

"Was it done thoroughly?" inquired the banker ironically.

"A thorough ducking?" gasped his son and heir. "I should say it was thorough, sir!"

"Then I wish that the incident would make sufficient impression on you to last you a few days," went on Mr. Dodge bitterly. "I doubt it, however."

"Father, I want you to back me in having some of my assailants arrested for that ducking!"

"I shall do nothing of the sort," rejoined the banker. "The ridicule that this affair has brought upon my family has gone far enough already. You are my son, but a most foolish one, if not worse, and I feel that I am under obligations to the men or boys who carried you to the horse trough and endeavored to cure you of some of your folly."

"I had hoped, sir, that you would stand back of your own son better than that. I am positive that Mr. Bayliss will not allow the outrage to pass unnoticed. I believe that Mr. Bayliss will take stern measures to avenge the great insult to his son."

"What Mr. Bayliss may do is Mr. Bayliss' affair, not mine," replied the banker coolly. "Is young Bayliss in this house at present?"

"Yes, sir; he's at the dinner table."

"Then I won't urge you to be inhospitable, Bert, let him finish his dinner in peace. After dinner, however, the sooner young Bayliss returns to his home, or at least, goes away from here, the better I shall be pleased. As for you, young man, I have had enough of your actions. I have a nice, and very quiet, summer place in mind where I am going to send you to-morrow. You will stay there, too, unless you wish to incur my severe displeasure. I will tell you about your new plans for the summer after breakfast to-morrow, young man."

"You're always hard on me," grumbled Bert sullenly. "But what do you think about Dick Prescott and his friends?"

"As for young Prescott," replied the banker, "he is altogether above your class, Bert. You should leave him severely alone. Don't allow yourself to attempt anything against Prescott, Reade, Darrin, or any of that crowd. You will find that any one of them has too much brains for you to hope to cope with. I repeat that you are not at all in their class as to brains, and it is quite time that you recognize the fact. Now, you may return to your dinner. Be good enough to tell your mother that I will be at table within fifteen minutes. Present my apologies to your mother for not having been more prompt. Now---go!"

Bert Dodge left his father with the feeling that he resembled an unjustly whipped dog.

"So I've got to go away and rusticate somewhere for the summer, have I?" wondered Bert angrily. "And all on account of such a gang of muckers as the fellows who call themselves Dick & Co.!"

Nor did young Bayliss fare any better on his return home that night. He, too, was ordered away for the remainder of the summer by his father, who had just returned from abroad, nor was he allowed to accompany Bert Dodge.

What of Dick & Co. during all this time?

They had gone away on an avowed fishing trip and they were making the most of it.

Harry Hazelton attended to perch fishing, when any of those fish were wanted. Tom Reade and Dan made the most of the black bass sport, while Dick, with Dave and Greg as under-studies, went after trout.

Several trips were made down to the St. Clair Lake House, and on each occasion large quantities of bass and trout were sold to the proprietor. He took all their offerings.

As a result of the sales of trout and bass some substantial money orders were forwarded to the elder Prescott, to be cashed by Dick on his return.

One afternoon Dick, who had gone trout fishing alone, returned with so small a string of the speckled ones that some of Tom's bass had to be added to the supper that night.

"I've been doing rather an unsportsmanlike thing, I fear," admitted Dick.

"Then 'fess up!" ordered Tom Reade.

"The trout are beginning to bite poorly," Prescott went on. "The fact is, we've all but cleaned up the stream."

"There must be a few hundred pounds left there yet," guessed Dave.

"There may be, and I hope there are," Prescott went on, "but I've decided not to take any more trout out of the stream this year. Whatever are now left in the stream we must leave for next summer. No good sportsman would ever deplete a stream of all its trout."

"The bass are still biting fairly well," mused Tom aloud. "However, they're not as easy to catch as they were. Had we better leave the bass alone, also?"

"We might take out what bass we want to eat," Dick suggested, "but not attempt to catch any more than that this summer."

"Too bad," muttered Tom. "I was in hopes that we were going to put by a big stake in the bank, to be divided later on."

"We already have money enough for our purpose," Dick suggested. "We have sufficient funds to take us all away on a fine jaunt during August, and these are the last days of July, now."

"I hate to go away from this lake," muttered Dave.

"It has been very pleasant here," Prescott agreed, "and if the rest of you vote for it, I'll agree to put in the rest of our summer vacation hereabouts."

"No," dissented Tom. "I reckon change of scene and air is as good for us as it is for other folks."

"Tom wants to get where he can find more bass fishing," Greg laughed.

"I've had enough of that sport to last me for one summer," retorted Reade.

The day was closing in a gorgeous sunset. In fifteen minutes more the sun would be down, but there would still be left the long July twilight.

"Did any of you ever see a more beautiful summer day than this has been?" asked Harry Hazelton presently.

"I haven't anything to offer in the line of such experience," Tom confessed.

"There are some days," Hazelton went on half dreamily, "that somehow makes a fellow feel thoroughly contented with himself."

"That's the way I feel to-night," Tom admitted, with an indolent air.

"I'd be contented if I knew one thing, and I suspect that you fellows might be able to tell me, if you only would."

None noticed the twinkle in Prescott's eyes as he spoke.

"I'll offer!" cried Tom good-humoredly. "If it's anything I can tell you, I'll do it."

"S-t-u-n-g!" spelled Dick slowly.

Tom suddenly sat up, glaring suspiciously at his chum.

"Now, what have I let myself in for?" demanded Reade.

"You gave your word you'd tell me, if you could, Tom," Dick went on, "and no one else can tell me nearly as well as you can. What I want to know is this: What happened to you, that night a few weeks ago, when you broke a bottle under my window, and then started down the street as fast as you could go with a crowd of Gridley folks behind you?"

"You promised!" chorused the other four boys.

"Well, if that isn't a low-down way to dig out of me what is purely my own business!" exclaimed Tom Reade, with a scowl.

Nevertheless Tom, like the other members of Dick & Co., had a high idea of the sacredness of his word, so, after a sigh, he went on:

"When I ran away from your window, Dick, with that pack of people behind me, I dashed into a full-fledged scrape that was none of mine. You know that Mr. Ritchie, whom some of the Central Grammar boys plague so fearfully, just because he always gets so mad and makes such threats against all boys in general?

"Well, it seems that, while I was helping Timmy Finbrink out of his difficulties, and afterwards tried to fool you with the fake window-breaking, some of the Central fellows had been down at Ritchie's playing tick-tack on one of his front windows. Tick-tack is a stupid game, and it got me into a mess that night.

"It seems that Mr. Ritchie had already been bothered that evening before the

Central fellows began, and he had telephoned to a friend down the street who had two college boys visiting him. So the friend and the two college fellows went out, on their way to Mr. Ritchie's. Then he heard the tapping on his window again, and Mr. Ritchie ran out through the front door. The fellows who had been doing the trick had just time to drop behind a flower bed.

"I had shaken off the crowd that started after me from Main Street, and had turned the corner down that side street. As luck would have it, I had just passed the Ritchie gate when Mr. Ritchie opened his front door. He thought I was the offender, and started after me, yelling to me to stop. Just for the exercise I kept on running, though not so fast, for I wanted to see how far Mr. Ritchie would chase me. And then I ran straight into the friend and the two college boys.

"Those college boys tried to collar me. I was foolish enough to stop and tackle. I had one of them on his back, and was doing nicely with the other, when the two men joined in. I was down and being held hard, while Mr. Ritchie was threatening to have me sent to jail for life---for something I hadn't done, mind you!

"As I ran by the Ritchie yard I saw the three Central Grammar School boys hiding behind the flower bed. It made me mad, I suppose, to think that college boys, who aren't real men, anyway, should stoop so low as to try to catch a lot of grammar school prankers, so I fought back at my captors with some vim. Of course I got the worst of it, including the bruise on my cheek, but I mussed those two college boys up a bit, too. Then, when I got on my feet, the two college boys still holding me, I demanded virtuously to know what it was all about. Mr. Ritchie explained hotheadedly. I told him I could prove that I had just come from Main Street, but my captors didn't let go of me until we came to Mr. Ritchie's. Then I saw at a glance that the Central fellows had made a good get-away, so then I told Mr. Ritchie how the trick had been done against him. I showed him just how the string had been rigged, and pointed out the spot where the Central boys had flopped down behind the flower bed. Their footprints were there in the soil to show it. By this time all hands were ready to believe that a high school senior hadn't been up to such baby stuff, and Mr. Ritchie apologized to me. I was pretty stiff about it, though, and told Mr. Ritchie that I would consult with my parents before I'd decide to let such an outrageous assault pass without making trouble for my assailants."

"What did your folks say about it?" pressed Danny Grin eagerly.

"Dalzell, aren't you the little innocent?" asked Reade, with good-humored scorn. "Of course I never said anything to my folks about such a foolish adventure as that. But I'll wager that I left Mr. Ritchie worried for just the next few days. Now, you fellows know the whole yarn---and I don't think much of Dick's way of buncoing me out of it, either."

"Don't all turn at once," said Dave in a very low tone, "but, behind you, through the fork in the cleft rock, the Man with the Haunting Face is staring this way. Be careful, and we may-----"

But, as if shot from spring guns, all five of the others were up on their feet and running fast toward that strange man who had furnished their lake mystery without solving it.

## CHAPTER XXIII
## "FOUR OF US ARE PIN-HEADS!"

Oh, you fellows have spoiled it!" groaned Dave as he joined last of all in the chase.

From the tent to the cleft rock was perhaps a hundred and twenty yards.

For such sprinters as these members of the Gridley High School eleven it did not require much time to cover the distance. Yet, by the time that Danny Grin, in the lead, had reached the further side of the rock there was no sign of the presence of the Man with the Haunting Face.

"You dreamed it, Dave," charged Greg Holmes.

"No, I didn't, either," muttered Darrin, joining the group of puzzled youngsters. "I saw the face as plainly and positively as I see any of your faces."

"It's hard to believe that," muttered Tom, shaking his head.

"I was wide awake, and my eyesight is good," Darry insisted.

"Then where has your man gone?" asked Dick. "If he had run to any point near here we would have found him."

Dave Darrin began to pry about, looking for some concealed opening near the base of the cleft, rock. He explored diligently, but could find no such clue as he had hoped.

"Nonsense! I'm going back to camp," declared Tom Reade.

"So'm I," Hazelton agreed.

"Dave can't have been mistaken," offered Greg.

"Thank you for one trusting soul," said Dave gratefully.

"But one thing I do know," Greg went on.

"What?" asked Darry.

"Even if our strange fellow was here, he is here no longer, and moreover, he

has succeeded in getting away without leaving any trace," young Holmes continued. "So I'm going to join the delegation that returns to camp."

Only Dick and Dave were left standing there by the cleft rock.

The sun had sunk below the horizon, but the light was still strong.

"If you fellows had taken it easily, as I asked," complained Dave, "we might
have gotten hold of that elusive chap. To me he looked hungry. I thought he was
eyeing our camp longingly, as though he'd like to stroll down and ask us for food.
But that startling charge of the light brigade must have bewildered or frightened
him---and so he went up in smoke, as he has always done when we've sighted him."

"It wouldn't surprise me if we could find which way he has gone," whispered
Prescott.

"What do you mean?"

"Look where I'm pointing with the toe of my boot," Dick went on.

"I'm looking."

"Do you see anything?"

"The earth."

"Look harder!"

Down went Darry to his knees.

"Look out," warned Dick, "or you'll obliterate it."

"And I was bragging of my good eyesight," grunted Darry. "Why, this is a foot-
print, and none of our crowd saw it."

"Besides, it's the print of a bare foot," Prescott went on. "You see the way in
which it is pointing?"

"Yes; toward that patch of low bushes yonder. But our chap couldn't have run
through those low bushes, or we'd have seen him."

"Yes; if he had been holding himself erect."

"Or even had he crouched and run," Dave affirmed.

"Dave Darrin, you've played baseball, if my recollection serves me correctly."

"Of course."

"Did you ever slide for a base?"

"What-----"

"Or see anyone else slide for base?"

"Then our man-----"

"He held himself low and ran as far as the bushes," Dick went on. "Then he fell and slid for it through the low bushes. See, here's the second print of a bare foot, and the direction is the same."

"Don't tell our mutton-head chums about it," Darrin begged. "Let's follow it up ourselves."

"All right," nodded Dick; "but if we find our fellow, don't let him suspect that we've reached his hiding place and know it. We'll just see what we can find out, and not give ourselves away."

"Go ahead," begged Darry.

"Remember, I'm not certain that we can find the fellow's hiding place before dark. It may be some distance from here. We'll try, though, and hope for luck."

Dick sauntered easily along in the direction indicated by the two footprints.

As they entered the patch of low bushes both boys noted the fact that the ground had been slightly disturbed, as it might have been by the sliding of a human body over it.

Dick, whose eyes were keener, easily followed the marks on the ground. Indeed, he did so without appearing to pay much heed to the earth under his feet.

Then the trailers passed three trees, behind which the escaping man might have found good cover.

A hundred yards further on Dave and Dick entered the edge of a grove of trees. Here there were also several rather thick tangles of brush and bush.

Well inside of one clump Dave, with a start, fancied he saw something that looked like a wall woven of green leaves. But Dick was trudging on ahead. Prescott continued in the lead for another quarter of a mile before he turned.

"You passed the one real sign," murmured Darry at last.

"I know I did," agreed Dick, "and we're going back wide of that place. You mean the jungle where you saw a bit of what looked like the brush-woven wall of a bush hut?"

"Yes," assented Darrin.

"It's a well-hidden place," declared Dick, "and I don't so much wonder that we didn't find it before. But now we'll go back to camp."

"And what next?"

"I don't know," Prescott confessed, looking puzzled. "We really haven't any right to pounce on the man unless we catch him doing something. Anyone has a right to lead the wild life in the woods, unless he's a criminal or a lunatic."

"My vote is that our chap is a lunatic," suggested Darry.

"If he is, then he's a harmless one, anyway. Let's go back, by a roundabout way, and tell the fellows."

"There are four pin-heads in this camp," was Tom Reade's decision, when he heard the report brought back by the others. "Only two of us have brains enough to see anything that's written right on the face of the earth."

"But what are we going to do about our man?" asked Greg.

"That's what we must figure out," Dick replied. "I don't see that we can do anything except send word to the authorities down in the village, and let them act as they see fit."

"What authorities are there in the village?" Dave inquired.

"I don't know. That we'll have to find out. We-----"

Dick paused suddenly, listening keenly.

"Do you fellows hear that?" he whispered.

"I hear a rumble of wheels off in the distance," replied Greg. "The air is so wonderfully still that sound carries a long way this evening."

Dick ran into the tent, returning with an envelope and a pad of paper.

"Come along, Dave," Dick requested. "And you'd better bring Tom's flashlight. It will be dark before we get back."

The battery of the flashlight having had a good rest, now furnished an excellent light again.

As the two chums set off at a trot Greg inquired:

"Now what are that pair up to?"

"Being one of the four pin-heads belonging to this outfit," Tom made solemn reply, "I can only guess."

"Then what's your guess?" quizzed Danny Grin.

"From the sound that wagon makes rolling over the rough road," Tom answered, "I judge that it's headed for the village. If it is, Dick is going to send in a note by the driver, and thus save one or two of us the tiresome sixteen-mile round trip."

Which proved to be a very correct guess, for Prescott and Darrin, returning three quarters of an hour later, informed the others that Dick had halted the driver, asking the farmer to wait while the note was being written.

"I sent the note to the post-master," Dick. went on. "If he and the other folks in the village take enough interest in the matter, I imagine a constable will be sent up to-morrow."

"Perhaps to-night," hinted Dalzell.

"If you were a constable," asked Tom, "would you want to be pulled out of your bed and sent on such a trip in the night time?"

"I'll tell you one thing that we fellows want to do," hinted Darrin, a few minutes later. "When we go to bed we want to take pains to leave some food where it can be easily borrowed by our man of mystery. I've an idea that he has been making night trips down here once in a while to obtain something to eat."

"Two or three times I've thought I missed food in the morning," nodded Greg. "Yet, if our man has been getting all his food here, then he is a very light eater."

"And welcome to the little he borrowed," Dick finished.

"Drowsiness is overcoming curiosity for me," yawned Reade, as he rose and strolled toward the tent. "Any of you other fellows going to turn in?"

"I will," yawned Dalzell, "if you'll permit me to sleep in the same tent with you."

Fifteen minutes later all of the high school boys were sound asleep. They all dreamed that night of the Man with the Haunting Face.

# CHAPTER XXIV
## CONCLUSION

Where's that man you wanted us to look at?" demanded a farmer whose trousers were tucked into his boots.

It was about ten o'clock the next forenoon when this man, accompanied by another man with the same kind of boottops, strode into the camp of Dick & Co.

"Are you a constable from the village, sir?" inquired young Prescott.

"No; we haven't any constable in the village," replied the farmer, chewing at a straw. "I'm the Overseer of the Poor."

"We'll take you to where we think the man is hiding," Dick replied. "Tom and Dave, suppose you two hurry ahead of us, around the woods, and stand where you can head our man of mystery off in case he tries to run the other way. Dave knows where the place is."

Reade and Darrin promptly departed.

"We can start in two or three minutes from now, after they get in position, if that suits you, sir," Dick suggested.

"Suits me," nodded the Overseer of the Poor. "I'm in no great hurry. Snug camp you boys have here."

"We've enjoyed ourselves greatly," Dick admitted.

"Going to stay here long?"

"No, sir; we're due back in Gridley soon."

After a little more chat Dick stated that he believed it was time to go forward to the hut in the woods.

He and Greg went, accompanied by the two farmers. All four trod stealthily. Prescott, in advance, went straight to the bushes that surrounded the brush hut.

Still in the lead, Dick, found the doorway, screened by a tattered blanket, pushed it aside and peered in.

On the floor of earth lay the Man with the Haunting Face. He was so still that at first Dick thought him dead. Dick motioned to the others to come forward.

"Humph!" grunted the Overseer of the Poor. "That's Ed Hoskins, who lives over Pelham way."

At sound of the voice the sleeping man quivered, opened his eyes, then, with a scream, sat up, trembling violently.

"You've got me!" he screamed. "You've found me---and I'm not yet fit to go!"

Dick stepped aside to let the farmers in, while Darrin and Reade approached the spot at a run.

"Keep quiet, Hoskins," ordered the Overseer of the Poor. "Quiet, man; I tell you!"

"Oh, I didn't mean to do it!" moaned the unhappy captive. "I didn't mean to do it, I tell  you! And now I must lose my life before I'm fit to go."

"'Touched' here," murmured Prescott, tapping his forehead.

"What are you making such a fuss about, Ed Hoskins?" demanded the Overseer of the Poor.

"I never meant to harm my wife!" screamed Hoskins in an agony of fear. "We had had words, and I meant nothing but to push her aside so I could pass. But she fell downstairs. It wasn't my fault that her neck was broken!"

"Whose neck was broken?" demanded the farmer.

"My wife's. But I never meant to do it."

"Humph!" remarked the Overseer of the Poor. "If your wife broke her neck, Ed Hoskins, she doesn't know it yet. She's doing some pretty husky work. She's the hired help over at St. Ingram's. She went there to work after you went away."

"Don't try to fool me," trembled Hoskins. "Don't! My wife's dead, and now I've got to go and pay the penalty of a crime I never meant to commit."

"What you need, Ed," observed the Overseer of the Poor, "is a bath, a couple of square meals, a little daylight, and a freight load of common horse sense. Come out of this place. We'll take you to your wife, and you'll find that she's very much alive, and heart-broken over your running away from her. She's fretting because she thinks her own conduct made you run away from her."

"I guess we don't belong here," murmured Dick to his chums. "Suppose we hurry down to the camp."

Five minutes later the two farmers also reached camp, holding Hoskins between them.

"It all shows what a man's fool way of reasoning---or, rather, not reasoning---can bring him to," explained the Overseer of the Poor in a low voice to the boys. "Ed Hoskins isn't exactly one of life's heavyweights, but he was always a good enough fellow, and industrious. He married a good-hearted, simple-minded girl, and they were mighty devoted to each other. But, back the last of May, Ed and his wife had a little bit of a tiff. They were standing near the top of the stairs in their house. Ed, according to his own story, went to push her aside so he could go downstairs, when his wife lost her balance and fell half way down the stairs. She fainted, I reckon, and Ed, in a great fright, thought she had broken her neck. So he ran down the stairs past her, got out of the house with a pair of blankets, a little food and a hatchet, and started up this miserable road in the night time. He says he knew he'd have to go to the electric chair some day for his deed, but he wanted to come up here and prepare his soul before he gave up his life. He says he got along all right until you boys came up here on purpose to find him and run him down for the law. He tells me that the first time some of you crossed the lake in a canoe he rigged up some bushes to a wooden frame, and swam, with his head inside the frame, hoping to get close to you and hear what you had to say about him. Then, he tells me, you moved your camp across the lake, and he knew you were here on the law's business. He says he has known, for certain, all along, that you'd get him sooner or later, but he couldn't get up the strength of mind to leave here. What I told Ed about his wife was true. She got nothing worse out of her fall than a bruise on one elbow. Gosh! Ed's wife will be as tickled to see him alive as he'll be to see her strong and well."

"Hoskins is a little touched in the upper story, isn't he?" Dick asked.

"Maybe he has been lately," replied the Overseer of the Poor. "But when he finds I haven't lied to him he'll be O.K. right away. Ed was never too strong in his mental works, but he's a good fellow, just the same, and he's bright enough for his trade---blacksmith's helper. Now, I guess I'd better be going back with him, for Ed will be all excitement and dread till he gets the first word from his wife. Miss. Hoskins wife be terribly obliged to you young men. I am, too, 'cause I'll be glad to see that couple together again. They're so fond of each other that they've no business apart. So I reckon, Master Prescott and the rest of you young men, we'll be a-going now."

The visitors had soon left the camp behind them. The last seen of Hoskins, he was walking with the dazed air of a man who knows he's dreaming and is mortally afraid to wake up.

But that same day Mr. and Mrs. Hoskins were reunited and began life anew together.

"It all goes to show," the Overseer of the Poor afterwards explained philosophically, "what a fool a fellow is to be afraid to go back and look at his work. It's the same spirit that makes automobile cowards afraid to stop the machine and go back to look at the child they've hit. Any fellow that's afraid to go back and look at his mistake is bound to be mainly unhappy in life."

A very few days afterwards Dick & Co., still propelling the push cart by turns, arrived in Gridley toward dark one late July evening.

They had so much to tell their relatives and friends that none of them got to bed very early on that occasion.

However, the month of August lay before them. These boys now planned the greatest summer vacation trip that they had ever enjoyed. Part of the trail of this vacation lay over in Tottenville.

So, by ten o'clock the next morning, Dick Prescott, alone, hurried up the side street on which he lived. Just as he neared the Main Street corner he beheld a trolley car labeled "Tottenville" pass the corner. Dick's shrill whistle rang out, but the conductor failed to hear it.

Away raced Dick in the wake of the speeding trolley car. Down the street for two blocks he dashed after it.

At first it looked as though the high school boy would overtake the car. But when he saw the car turn a corner and go off on the Tottenville road, young Prescott slowed down, panting and wiping his perspiring face.

"Hey!" called a man standing in a group of others on the curbstone. "Were you trying to catch that car."

"Was I trying to catch the car?" echoed Dick Prescott, his eyes opening wide in amazement. "No, sir! I made a wager that I could chase that car right off of Main

Street! And I won the bet," Dick added proudly. "You all saw me do it!"

Then, while the man who had asked the question reddened under the laughter of his companions, Prescott strolled slowly back up Main Street to watch for the next car bearing the "Tottenville" sign.

"Good morning, Prescott," came a greeting from Lawyer Ripley, just then coming out of a store. "How did you young men enjoy that collapsible canoe?"

"That canoe, sir? It made the vacation trip a perfect one. But were you the one who sent it, Mr. Ripley?"

"Yes," assented the lawyer, "though acting as agent for another. You remember how much Mr. Page wanted to do for you boys, after your splendid work for him last summer? Mr. Page wanted to do something for you this summer, and he and I hit upon the collapsible canoe as a remembrance so simple and inexpensive that you young men were quite likely to accept it."

"Mr. Ripley," begged Dick earnestly, "will you accept the very best thanks of us all for that canoe? And will you please convey our deepest gratitude to Mr. Page? We couldn't have had anything that would have delighted us as much."

Readers of the preceding volume of this series are well aware of the reason of Mr. Page's great gratitude to Dick & Co.

The next Tottenville car that came along had Dick Prescott for one of its passengers.

This narrative, however, has been finished. That trolley, to Tottenville really belongs to the next and final volume in this series, which is published under the title, "*The High School Boys' Training Hike; Or, Making Themselves 'Hard as Nails*."

This new story will be found to contain the full record of a most wonderful vacation jaunt taken by six young champions of the Gridley High School football squad.

Yet this jaunt did not consist wholly of training work, for Dick & Co. fell in with a lot of tremendously exciting adventures.

What these were and how Dick & Co. acted under amazingly strange circumstances will be set forth fully in that volume.

### The Codes Of Hammurabi And Moses
### W. W. Davies

QTY

The discovery of the Hammurabi Code is one of the greatest achievements of archaeology, and is of paramount interest, not only to the student of the Bible, but also to all those interested in ancient history...

**Religion**     **ISBN: *1-59462-338-4***          **Pages:132**

*MSRP $12.95*

### The Theory of Moral Sentiments
### Adam Smith

QTY

This work from 1749. contains original theories of conscience amd moral judgment and it is the foundation for systemof morals.

**Philosophy**  **ISBN: *1-59462-777-0***          **Pages:536**

*MSRP $19.95*

### Jessica's First Prayer
### Hesba Stretton

QTY

In a screened and secluded corner of one of the many railway-bridges which span the streets of London there could be seen a few years ago, from five o'clock every morning until half past eight, a tidily set-out coffee-stall, consisting of a trestle and board, upon which stood two large tin cans, with a small fire of charcoal burning under each so as to keep the coffee boiling during the early hours of the morning when the work-people were thronging into the city on their way to their daily toil...

**Pages:84**

**Childrens**   **ISBN: *1-59462-373-2***        *MSRP $9.95*

### My Life and Work
### Henry Ford

QTY

Henry Ford revolutionized the world with his implementation of mass production for the Model T automobile. Gain valuable business insight into his life and work with his own auto-biography... "We have only started on our development of our country we have not as yet, with all our talk of wonderful progress, done more than scratch the surface. The progress has been wonderful enough but..."

**Pages:300**

**Biographies/**    **ISBN: *1-59462-198-5***      *MSRP $21.95*

## The Art of Cross-Examination
## Francis Wellman

QTY

I presume it is the experience of every author, after his first book is published upon an important subject, to be almost overwhelmed with a wealth of ideas and illustrations which could readily have been included in his book, and which to his own mind, at least, seem to make a second edition inevitable. Such certainly was the case with me; and when the first edition had reached its sixth impression in five months, I rejoiced to learn that it seemed to my publishers that the book had met with a sufficiently favorable reception to justify a second and considerably enlarged edition. ...

**Pages:412**

Reference ISBN: *1-59462-647-2*   *MSRP $19.95*

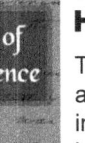

## On the Duty of Civil Disobedience
## Henry David Thoreau

QTY

Thoreau wrote his famous essay, On the Duty of Civil Disobedience, as a protest against an unjust but popular war and the immoral but popular institution of slave-owning. He did more than write—he declined to pay his taxes, and was hauled off to gaol in consequence. Who can say how much this refusal of his hastened the end of the war and of slavery ?

Law   ISBN: *1-59462-747-9*   **Pages:48**
*MSRP $7.45*

## Dream Psychology Psychoanalysis for Beginners
## Sigmund Freud

QTY

Sigmund Freud, born Sigismund Schlomo Freud (May 6, 1856 - September 23, 1939), was a Jewish-Austrian neurologist and psychiatrist who co-founded the psychoanalytic school of psychology. Freud is best known for his theories of the unconscious mind, especially those involving the mechanism of repression; his redefinition of sexual desire as mobile and directed towards a wide variety of objects; and his therapeutic techniques, especially his understanding of transference in the therapeutic relationship and the presumed value of dreams as sources of insight into unconscious desires.

**Pages:196**

Psychology   ISBN: *1-59462-905-6*   *MSRP $15.45*

## The Miracle of Right Thought
## Orison Swett Marden

QTY

Believe with all of your heart that you will do what you were made to do. When the mind has once formed the habit of holding cheerful, happy, prosperous pictures, it will not be easy to form the opposite habit. It does not matter how improbable or how far away this realization may see, or how dark the prospects may be, if we visualize them as best we can, as vividly as possible, hold tenaciously to them and vigorously struggle to attain them, they will gradually become actualized, realized in the life. But a desire, a longing without endeavor, a yearning abandoned or held indifferently will vanish without realization.

**Pages:360**

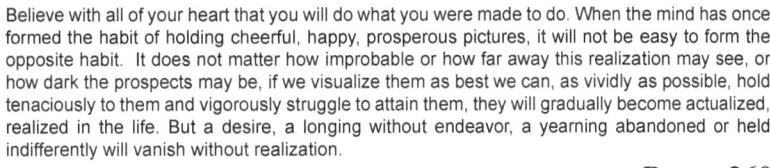

Self Help   ISBN: *1-59462-644-8*   *MSRP $25.45*

**www.bookjungle.com** *email: sales@bookjungle.com fax: 630-214-0564 mail: Book Jungle  PO Box 2226  Champaign, IL 61825*

QTY

**The Rosicrucian Cosmo-Conception Mystic Christianity** *by Max Heindel*  ISBN: *1-59462-188-8*  **$38.95**
*The Rosicrucian Cosmo-conception is not dogmatic, neither does it appeal to any other authority than the reason of the student. It is: not controversial, but is: sent forth in the, hope that it may help to clear...*  New Age/Religion Pages 646

**Abandonment To Divine Providence** *by Jean-Pierre de Caussade*  ISBN: *1-59462-228-0*  **$25.95**
*"The Rev. Jean Pierre de Caussade was one of the most remarkable spiritual writers of the Society of Jesus in France in the 18th Century. His death took place at Toulouse in 1751. His works have gone through many editions and have been republished...*  Inspirational/Religion Pages 400

**Mental Chemistry** *by Charles Haanel*  ISBN: *1-59462-192-6*  **$23.95**
*Mental Chemistry allows the change of material conditions by combining and appropriately utilizing the power of the mind. Much like applied chemistry creates something new and unique out of careful combinations of chemicals the mastery of mental chemistry...*  New Age Pages 354

**The Letters of Robert Browning and Elizabeth Barret Barrett 1845-1846 vol II**  ISBN: *1-59462-193-4*  **$35.95**
*by Robert Browning and Elizabeth Barrett*  Biographies Pages 596

**Gleanings In Genesis (volume I)** *by Arthur W. Pink*  ISBN: *1-59462-130-6*  **$27.45**
*Appropriately has Genesis been termed "the seed plot of the Bible" for in it we have, in germ form, almost all of the great doctrines which are afterwards fully developed in the books of Scripture which follow...*  Religion/Inspirational Pages 420

**The Master Key** *by L. W. de Laurence*  ISBN: *1-59462-001-6*  **$30.95**
*In no branch of human knowledge has there been a more lively increase of the spirit of research during the past few years than in the study of Psychology, Concentration and Mental Discipline. The requests for authentic lessons in Thought Control, Mental Discipline and...*  New Age/Business Pages 422

**The Lesser Key Of Solomon Goetia** *by L. W. de Laurence*  ISBN: *1-59462-092-X*  **$9.95**
*This translation of the first book of the "Lemegton" which is now for the first time made accessible to students of Talismanic Magic was done, after careful collation and edition, from numerous Ancient Manuscripts in Hebrew, Latin, and French...*  New Age/Occult Pages 92

**Rubaiyat Of Omar Khayyam** *by Edward Fitzgerald*  ISBN:*1-59462-332-5*  **$13.95**
*Edward Fitzgerald, whom the world has already learned, in spite of his own efforts to remain within the shadow of anonymity, to look upon as one of the rarest poets of the century, was born at Bredfield, in Suffolk, on the 31st of March, 1809. He was the third son of John Purcell...*  Music Pages 172

**Ancient Law** *by Henry Maine*  ISBN: *1-59462-128-4*  **$29.95**
*The chief object of the following pages is to indicate some of the earliest ideas of mankind, as they are reflected in Ancient Law, and to point out the relation of those ideas to modern thought.*  Religiom/History Pages 452

**Far-Away Stories** *by William J. Locke*  ISBN: *1-59462-129-2*  **$19.45**
*"Good wine needs no bush, but a collection of mixed vintages does. And this book is just such a collection. Some of the stories I do not want to remain buried for ever in the museum files of dead magazine-numbers an author's not unpardonable vanity..."*  Fiction Pages 272

**Life of David Crockett** *by David Crockett*  ISBN: *1-59462-250-7*  **$27.45**
*"Colonel David Crockett was one of the most remarkable men of the times in which he lived. Born in humble life, but gifted with a strong will, an indomitable courage, and unremitting perseverance...*  Biographies/New Age Pages 424

**Lip-Reading** *by Edward Nitchie*  ISBN: *1-59462-206-X*  **$25.95**
*Edward B. Nitchie, founder of the New York School for the Hard of Hearing, now the Nitchie School of Lip-Reading, Inc, wrote "LIP-READING Principles and Practice". The development and perfecting of this meritorious work on lip-reading was an undertaking...*  How-to Pages 400

**A Handbook of Suggestive Therapeutics, Applied Hypnotism, Psychic Science**  ISBN: *1-59462-214-0*  **$24.95**
*by Henry Munro*  Health/New Age/Health/Self-help Pages 376

**A Doll's House: and Two Other Plays** *by Henrik Ibsen*  ISBN: *1-59462-112-8*  **$19.95**
*Henrik Ibsen created this classic when in revolutionary 1848 Rome. Introducing some striking concepts in playwriting for the realist genre, this play has been studied the world over.*  Fiction/Classics/Plays 308

**The Light of Asia** *by sir Edwin Arnold*  ISBN: *1-59462-204-3*  **$13.95**
*In this poetic masterpiece, Edwin Arnold describes the life and teachings of Buddha. The man who was to become known as Buddha to the world was born as Prince Gautama of India but he rejected the worldly riches and abandoned the reigns of power when...*  Religion/History/Biographies Pages 170

**The Complete Works of Guy de Maupassant** *by Guy de Maupassant*  ISBN: *1-59462-157-8*  **$16.95**
*"For days and days, nights and nights, I had dreamed of that first kiss which was to consecrate our engagement, and I knew not on what spot I should put my lips..."*  Fiction/Classics Pages 240

**The Art of Cross-Examination** *by Francis L. Wellman*  ISBN: *1-59462-309-0*  **$26.95**
*Written by a renowned trial lawyer, Wellman imparts his experience and uses case studies to explain how to use psychology to extract desired information through questioning.*  How-to/Science/Reference Pages 408

**Answered or Unanswered?** *by Louisa Vaughan*  ISBN: *1-59462-248-5*  **$10.95**
*Miracles of Faith in China*  Religion Pages 112

**The Edinburgh Lectures on Mental Science (1909)** *by Thomas*  ISBN: *1-59462-008-3*  **$11.95**
*This book contains the substance of a course of lectures recently given by the writer in the Queen Street Hall, Edinburgh. Its purpose is to indicate the Natural Principles governing the relation between Mental Action and Material Conditions...*  New Age/Psychology Pages 148

**Ayesha** *by H. Rider Haggard*  ISBN: *1-59462-301-5*  **$24.95**
*Verily and indeed it is the unexpected that happens! Probably if there was one person upon the earth from whom the Editor of this, and of a certain previous history, did not expect to hear again...*  Classics Pages 380

**Ayala's Angel** *by Anthony Trollope*  ISBN: *1-59462-352-X*  **$29.95**
*The two girls were both pretty, but Lucy who was twenty-one who supposed to be simple and comparatively unattractive, whereas Ayala was credited, as her Bombwhat romantic name might show, with poetic charm and a taste for romance. Ayala when her father died was nineteen...*  Fiction Pages 484

**The American Commonwealth** *by James Bryce*  ISBN: *1-59462-286-8*  **$34.45**
*An interpretation of American democratic political theory. It examines political mechanics and society from the perspective of Scotsman James Bryce*  Politics Pages 572

**Stories of the Pilgrims** *by Margaret P. Pumphrey*  ISBN: *1-59462-116-0*  **$17.95**
*This book explores pilgrims religious oppression in England as well as their escape to Holland and eventual crossing to America on the Mayflower, and their early days in New England...*  History Pages 268

QTY

**The Fasting Cure** *by Sinclair Upton*                                    ISBN: *1-59462-222-1*   **$13.95**
*In the Cosmopolitan Magazine for May, 1910, and in the Contemporary Review (London) for April, 1910, I published an article dealing with my experiences in fasting. I have written a great many magazine articles, but never one which attracted so much attention...   New Age/Self Help/Health Pages 164*

**Hebrew Astrology** *by Sepharial*                                    ISBN: *1-59462-308-2*   **$13.45**
*In these days of advanced thinking it is a matter of common observation that we have left many of the old landmarks behind and that we are now pressing forward to greater heights and to a wider horizon than that which represented the mind-content of our progenitors...   Astrology Pages 144*

**Thought Vibration or The Law of Attraction in the Thought World**           ISBN: *1-59462-127-6*   **$12.95**
*by William Walker Atkinson*                                    *Psychology/Religion Pages 144*

**Optimism** *by Helen Keller*                                    ISBN: *1-59462-108-X*   **$15.95**
*Helen Keller was blind, deaf, and mute since 19 months old, yet famously learned how to overcome these handicaps, communicate with the world, and spread her lectures promoting optimism.  An inspiring read for everyone...   Biographies/Inspirational Pages 84*

**Sara Crewe** *by Frances Burnett*                                    ISBN: *1-59462-360-0*   **$9.45**
*In the first place, Miss Minchin lived in London. Her home was a large, dull, tall one, in a large, dull square, where all the houses were alike, and all the sparrows were alike, and where all the door-knockers made the same heavy sound...   Childrens/Classic Pages 88*

**The Autobiography of Benjamin Franklin** *by Benjamin Franklin*           ISBN: *1-59462-135-7*   **$24.95**
*The Autobiography of Benjamin Franklin has probably been more extensively read than any other American historical work, and no other book of its kind has had such ups and downs of fortune. Franklin lived for many years in England, where he was agent...   Biographies/History Pages 332*

| Name | |
| --- | --- |
| Email | |
| Telephone | |
| Address | |
| | |
| City, State ZIP | |

☐ **Credit Card**          ☐ **Check / Money Order**

| Credit Card Number | |
| --- | --- |
| Expiration Date | |
| Signature | |

*Please Mail to:   Book Jungle*
*PO Box 2226*
*Champaign, IL 61825*
*or Fax to:          630-214-0564*

## ORDERING INFORMATION

**web**: *www.bookjungle.com*
**email**: *sales@bookjungle.com*
**fax**: *630-214-0564*
**mail**: *Book Jungle  PO Box 2226  Champaign, IL 61825*
**or PayPal** *to sales@bookjungle.com*

*Please contact us for bulk discounts*

## DIRECT-ORDER TERMS

**20% Discount if You Order
Two or More Books**
Free Domestic Shipping!
Accepted: Master Card, Visa,
Discover, American Express